BOARDING SCHOOL MYSTERIES

betrayed

Other books in the growing Faithgirlz!™ Library

Boarding School Mysteries
Vanished (Book One)
Burned (Book Three)
Poisoned (Book Four)

The Sophie Series
Sophie's World (Book One)
Sophie's Secret (Book Two)
Sophie Under Pressure (Book Three)
Sophie Steps Up (Book Four)
Sophie's First Dance (Book Five)
Sophie's Stormy Summer (Book Six)
Sophie's Friendship Fiasco (Book Seven)
Sophie and the New Girl (Book Eight)
Sophie Flakes Out (Book Nine)
Sophie Loves Jimmy (Book Ten)
Sophie's Drama (Book Eleven)
Sophie Gets Real (Book Twelve)

The Lucy Series
Lucy Doesn't Wear Pink (Book One)
Lucy Out of Bounds (Book Two)
Lucy's "Perfect" Summer (Book Three)
Lucy Finds Her Way (Book Four)

Other books by Kristi Holl
What's A Girl to Do?
Shine on, Girl!: Devotions to Keep You Sparkling
Girlz Rock: Devotions for You
Chick Chat: More Devotions for Girls
No Boys Allowed: Devotions for Girls

Check out www.faithgirlz.com

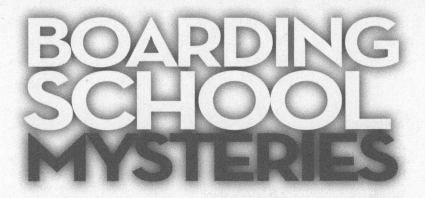

betrayed

Formerly titled *Secrets for Sale*

Kristi Holl

ZONDERKIDZ

Betrayed
Copyright © 2008, 2011 by Kristi Holl
Formerly titled *Secrets for Sale*

This title is also available as a Zondervan ebook.
Visit www.zondervan.com/ebooks.

Requests for information should be addressed to:

Zonderkidz, 3900 *Sparks Drive SE, Grand Rapids, Michigan 49546*

Library of Congress Cataloging-in-Publication Data

Holl, Kristi.
    [Secrets for sale]
    Betrayed / by Kristi Holl.
       p.   cm. — (Faithgirlz) (Boarding school mysteries ; bk. 2)
    Originally published in 2008 under the title, Secrets for sale.
    ISBN 978-0-310-72093-5 (softcover)
    [1. Boarding schools—Fiction. 2. Schools—Fiction. 3. Extortion—Fiction.
    4. Christian life—Fiction. 5. Mystery and detective stories.] I. Title.
    PZ7.H7079Bet 2011
    [Fic]—dc22   2010037924

Art direction and cover design: Sarah Molegraaf
Interior design: Carlos Eluterio Estrada

So we fix our eyes not on what is seen, but what is unseen.
For what is seen is temporary, but what is unseen is eternal.
— 2 Corinthians 4:18

table of contents

1
the threat

Damp musty air hovered over the historic theater's orchestra pit. Notebook in hand, Jeri McKane carefully stepped around the six-foot pit, mounted the stage steps, and slipped behind the plush red curtain. Backstage in the cavernous gloom, she picked her way around props, stools, and other obstacles. Squinting, she read the antique movie posters in plastic cases hung on the putrid green walls: *Birth of a Nation ... Cleopatra ... The Bells of St. Mary's.*

She tripped over a coiled rope and narrowly escaped landing on a papier-mâché horse and pumpkin coach. She was at Monday night's rehearsal in order to write an article about the spring play, a Rodgers and Hammerstein version of *Cinderella.* Jeri's roommate, Rosa Sanchez, was the star. Although only a sixth grader, Rosa's voice at try-outs had been the strongest by far. Onstage or off, she had a bubbly flair for the dramatic, and she'd been a natural choice for the lead.

Glancing across the small stage to the opposite wing, Jeri spotted Rosa. She started to call to her best friend but then paused, struck by Rosa's odd expression. Bent forward, Rosa looked as though she'd been hit in the stomach. Rosa covered her mouth with a shaking hand as she read a note.

What in the world was wrong?

Rosa hurriedly stuffed the paper in her purse. Jeri started toward her, but Rosa straightened and moved to center stage, her lips pressed into a thin line.

Frowning, Jeri reluctantly focused on her original goal. Turning, she found the set designers stretching material across a wooden frame. Painted on it were streaks of moonlight and village houses with glowing windows.

"Cool painting." Jeri reached out to touch it, but—unbalanced—she leaned her weight on one corner.

"Don't!" shouted a husky girl with a red bandana covering her hair. "It's wet!"

"Sorry," Jeri said, fingertips covered in blue paint. "I can't see back here." She looked for something to wipe her hands on and then finally used her jeans. "That really is beautiful."

"It *was* before you pulled it loose from the flat." Bandana Girl yanked on the chain of an overhead light. It swung back and forth, causing shadows to jump and leap across the stage. She touched up the smear with the tail of her T-shirt and then stretched the material and re-tacked it to the corner.

"Hey, I'm writing an article for the paper," Jeri explained, trying to sound important. "What's that wooden thing called again?"

"A flat." The girl pointed to other scenery painted on screens suspended from the ceiling. "Those are called backdrops. You raise and lower them with pulleys." Her eyes glinted. *"Don't touch the pulleys."*

"No problem," Jeri said.

Jeri turned in a slow circle. Although it smelled musty, she loved the old theater at the Landmark School for Girls. The restored theater was on the National Register of Historic Places, and it felt like a museum.

Without warning, someone grabbed Jeri's arm and she jumped. It was Britney, a seventh grader, who had appeared out of nowhere. "Rosa said you're writing about the play for the paper. Wait till you hear my song with Hailey. It's *hilarious.* You'll *love* 'Stepsisters' Lament.' I play Esmerelda, and Hailey is Prunella." She tapped Jeri's notebook. "You want to write that down?"

"Um. Okay."

"Really, someone ought to write a whole musical starring Esmerelda. We need to hear the other side of the story! Don't you think so?" Britney shook her cascading blonde hair that reached to her elbows.

Jeri remembered from tryouts that Britney had auditioned for the lead. "It's hard to imagine you as an ugly stepsister."

"Stage makeup!" Britney squatted, dug into a back-pack on the floor, and then handed Jeri two 4" x 6" glossy photos. "Keep these for your article. Isn't that some transformation?"

"No kidding." In the first photo Britney was her normal beautiful self. The second photo showed her in stage makeup. Britney-as-Esmerelda had a wart on her nose, a protruding chin, whiskers poking from several moles, and a scraggly black wig.

Britney grabbed Jeri's pen and wrote in her notebook. "My name ends in *ey*. B-r-i-t-n-e-y B-r-o-w-n. Let's get the publicity right."

"Thanks," Jeri said, thinking, *Cool!* Apparently, Rosa hadn't mentioned that Jeri's article was only for their sixth-grade media project, not for the official school paper, the Landmark *Lightning Bolt.*

"Let's go!" the director said, clapping her hands. "Ready, Cinderella? We'll do 'In My Own Little Corner.' "

Turning, Jeri skirted the scenery and props and hurried down the steps to take a front-row-center seat. She glanced around the stage and finally spotted Miss Kimberly down in the orchestra pit. Only her head, thick neck, and beefy raised arms were visible. The obese twenty-something woman was an enthusiastic drama coach, but she looked more like a sumo wrestler.

Onstage, Cinderella was "locked up" in a tower room to perform her next song. Earlier, she and Salli Hall (who played Prince Charming) had both been totally convincing in their duet—despite their matching blue uniform jumpers. Jeri couldn't wait until her friends could perform in costume.

Jeri gave Rosa a thumbs-up, but her roommate didn't respond. Instead, Rosa stared into space. *What's up?* Jeri wondered.

A musical introduction blared over the loudspeakers, startling Rosa. She missed her cue by a couple of beats, and when she came in, her voice was weak. Jeri could barely hear her. In a thin, thready soprano, Rosa sang about her own little corner of the world and being whatever she wanted to be. Woodenly, she moved back and forth in front of the tower windows.

Jeri sat forward. *What's the deal?*

At the end of the song, Jeri clapped and whistled. Rosa stood with shoulders sagging. Miss Kimberly, dressed in black Spandex pants and a ruffled pink tent top, laboriously climbed the stairs from the orchestra pit to the stage. She closed her eyes for a moment, as if dizzy, and then lumbered over to the tower setting and spoke quietly to Rosa. Judging by the look on Rosa's embarrassed face, the comments weren't good.

"—and when you hit this part," Miss Kimberly said, raising her voice, "your body language and tone of voice need to match the words and meaning of the song. Here.

Like this." She sat down on the child-size footstool, and it disappeared beneath her hulking frame. Although she sang the song without accompaniment and hit every note clear and true, she was breathless and pale at the end.

In the wings, Britney and Hailey snickered as the drama teacher sang about her own little chair. Jeri thought it was mean to laugh, but Miss Kimberly *did* need something more than a tiny chair.

Miss Kimberly's finger combed her short, curly hair and announced, "Rosa needs to try on her ball gown, but the rest of you can leave now." She yawned and rubbed her eyes. "Good job, everyone."

Cast members gathered up books, jackets, and backpacks. Jeri ran up the steps to the stage area, waited for Miss Kimberly to go ahead, and followed Rosa to the dressing room. "Are you sick? What's the matter?" she asked outside the door.

"Nothing."

"Come on, Rosa. What gives?" She blocked the doorway. "You always have more energy than everyone else put together. What happened?"

Rosa's eyes glistened with tears. "My song stunk!"

"Not true," Jeri said. "You didn't miss a note."

Head down, Rosa pushed past her into the dressing room. Jeri followed, still worried. The dressing room was done in red and white: a red wicker couch, two white wicker rockers, and a red wicker changing screen. Miss

Kimberly held up a pink and white sequined gown hanging on a padded hanger.

"Sweet dress!" Jeri said.

Rosa studied it doubtfully. "It looks awfully small."

Miss Kimberly slipped the dress off its hanger. "Try it on."

Rosa took the dress behind the changing screen.

"I'll help," Jeri said, following her.

"I can do it myself."

"You need someone to zip it."

Rosa was silent as Jeri helped her into the dress. Layers of a pink taffeta slip made the skirt stand out, but Rosa was right about the fit.

"Suck in," Jeri whispered, trying to close the back zipper. Rosa held her breath. "Suck *way* in."

"I *am*!"

Jeri tugged on the zipper, but it wouldn't budge. She feared ripping it loose from the fabric if she kept yanking on it.

"Come out when you're dressed," Miss Kimberly called.

Rosa rolled her eyes and then stepped out, holding the unzipped bodice up in front of her. "It's beautiful, but way too tiny. Maybe I could lose weight before opening night."

Jeri shook her head. "You *don't* need to lose weight."

"Anyway," the director said, "that's less than two weeks away. Losing weight isn't that easy." Miss Kimberly slapped her own bulging thighs as she heaved herself up from a rocker. Breathing hard, she circled the ball gown, examining the side and back seams, tugging here and jerking there. "Someone took this in several inches," she said. "The last person to wear this costume must have been skin and bones. The seams can be let back out."

Rosa twisted sideways to look. "Man, there's enough extra material for someone humongous."

The director caught her breath. A tremor passed through her, and then her hands were motionless as they rested on the satiny fabric.

Rosa's eyes widened in horror. "I didn't mean *you*, Miss Kimberly. I meant someone *really* big."

Eyes wide, Jeri glanced at Rosa. She meant well, but what a lie! Miss Kimberly weighed at least three or four hundred pounds.

"Well," Jeri added, trying to sound convincing, "you're so pretty that no one notices,"

Miss Kimberly's hands dropped to her sides, and she tugged on her pink tent top.

Rosa nodded. "And you're a lot of fun!"

"Don't worry, girls." Miss Kimberly forced a smile. "My size honestly isn't a problem. I can do whatever I want. If I wasn't swamped directing this play, I'd be in the community theater production in town. They're doing *Okalahoma!* It required some dancing as well as singing, and despite my bad knees, I got the part."

"Cool," Jeri said, flabbergasted at the idea of Miss Kimberly dancing onstage.

"I found I couldn't manage both plays at once though. The practice times overlapped. Maybe next time."

Jeri sighed, relieved the teacher's feelings didn't seem hurt.

Miss Kimberly glanced at her watch. "It's nearly seven thirty. Better change and get back to your dorm. Just leave the dress, and I'll get it resized." She smiled at Rosa. "Don't worry about it tonight. *Cinderella* will be a smashing success."

Rosa gave a half smile back and ducked behind the screen to change.

"I left my notebook in the front row," Jeri called. "Meet you by the back door." A minute later, Jeri spotted Rosa rushing to the exit. "Wait up!" She grabbed her coat, shrugged into the sleeves, and snatched up her backpack. When she got outside, Rosa was already half a block ahead. "Wait!" Jeri called again.

Rosa picked up speed, and Jeri finally slowed to a walk, bending into the stiff March wind. Her roommate obviously wanted to be alone, but why? Was she upset about the ball gown being so tight? Or Miss Kimberly's criticism of her song? Maybe it had something to do with the note she was reading before practice. Whatever it was, Jeri intended to find out the minute she got back to Hampton House.

She hurried down the dark sidewalk, barely aware of the carillon bells echoing from the bell tower across the frigid campus. She felt sorry for whichever frostbitten music student was playing the carillon keyboard tonight.

Five minutes later, Jeri opened the heavy door of the sixth-grade dorm and stepped inside. Warm cinnamon-scented air enveloped her, driving away the damp chill in her bones. She flung her coat on the hall tree and kicked off her wet shoes onto the rug. Passing the study room, she spotted her friends Abby and Nikki studying by the fire.

"Want a biscuit?" Abby asked, holding out a sugar cookie to Jeri. Abby was from Bath, England, and Jeri loved her accent. "Was practice beastly? Rosa ran upstairs without saying a word."

"Like she had blinders on," Nikki agreed. She leaned back and crossed her ankles, admiring her leather cowboy boots.

"Something's up with her." Jeri took the cookie from Abby and started toward her dorm room. She was halfway up the steps when Miss Barbara, the house mother's assistant, popped out of the kitchen doorway.

"You have mail, Jeri," she called, waving a letter.

"Really?" Jeri leaned over the banister for it and read the return address with disbelief. Her dad? "Thanks," she finally said, heading back upstairs.

Thoughts tumbled in her brain. Why was he contacting her *now*?

He'd dropped out of her life when she started at Landmark Hills last fall. Even when she went home to Iowa for winter break, he hadn't seen or called her. She couldn't believe he'd actually forgotten her at Christmas. He'd been on a cruise to the Bahamas with his girlfriend—some ditz named Sabrina. He'd promised to mail some gifts to Jeri, but no presents—or explanation—ever arrived.

Her mom had warned Jeri to expect Dad and Sabrina to get married, so Jeri dreaded reading the news in this letter. Taking a deep breath, she opened the letter, skimmed it, and broke into a grin. *Whoa!* Her dad *wasn't* getting married. He wanted to come for a visit—this weekend!

Apparently, he and Sabrina had broken up. *Thank heaven!* The last thing Jeri needed was a twenty-five-year-old stepmom. In the letter, her dad said he really missed Jeri and wanted to spend time with her. She'd been waiting all year for him to say that.

Slowly the smile faded, however, and her heart sank. Wait a minute! Her dad didn't miss *her.* He was just between girlfriends and feeling lonely. So *now* he had time to come for a visit. *Now* he wanted to see her. Anger burned in her chest. *Talk about unfair! Where was he when I needed* him? Well, maybe she didn't have time for *him* now. She had her newspaper writing and her friends.

She took several deep breaths. She'd answer him soon, but right now Rosa needed her.

Down the hall, Jeri paused outside their room before opening the door slowly. Rosa stood by the window, staring out into the darkness. Jeri could see her tormented expression reflected in the window pane.

"Rosa?" Jeri came in and closed the door behind her. "What's wrong?"

Rosa threw a wadded paper on her bed. "*This* is what's wrong."

Jeri smoothed out the note and read aloud: "You weren't in church on Sunday; you were in the park with Kevin. The headmistress doesn't know—yet. If you want to keep it that way, I want $20. Bring the money to the girls' restroom in the dining hall. Hide it in the garbage can on Tuesday by noon."

Jeri glanced up. "You're being *blackmailed*? No way you're doing this!"

"Like I have a choice."

Jeri read the note again. Last Sunday, Jeri didn't go to church because she wasn't feeling well, but Rosa had gone. She'd told Jeri afterward about her impulsive decision to skip church and walk along the creek with Kevin instead. They were just friends—Kevin went to the nearby boys' school—but Jeri knew Rosa could get in a lot of trouble for it.

"If you pay, Rosa, the blackmailer will ask for more later. It's always like that in the movies."

Rosa sat down on the silver radiator, her fingers clenched into fists. "What else can I do? This creep threatens to squeal if I don't."

Jeri frowned. At the very least, Rosa would get a reprimand and the school would call her missionary parents.

Rosa sniffed back her tears. "I could get expelled."

"Don't give the blackmailer money though. Give me a chance to help you first," Jeri said, touching Rosa's arm. "Maybe I could set a trap and catch him ... or her—it *must* be a girl if she's going to get the money from the girls' bathroom."

"And why would *you* want to catch the creep?"

Jeri frowned. "What's that supposed to mean? I want to help you!"

"I think you just want to report on it for your little newspaper and be a hero!"

"You really think that?!" Jeri cried, shocked.

Tears filled Rosa's eyes and spilled over, running down her cheeks. "You're the only person I told about going to the park with Kevin."

"But lots of people could have seen you. Or maybe Kevin told someone. Or—"

"I thought I could *trust* you," Rosa said.

Jeri stared at her. "What are you saying?"

"*You* wrote the note! I saw you backstage before my song." Rosa grabbed the paper. "Is that when you put this in my purse?"

2
blackmail

Jeri stood there—stunned and with her mouth hanging open—for several seconds. "I would never black-mail you!" she protested. "I can't believe you said that! You're my best friend."

Rosa made no comment.

"Why would I do such a thing?"

"You're jealous."

"*Of Kevin Mahoney?*" Jeri nearly choked. In her opinion, Rosa's friend was the most stuck-up kid at Landmark Hills Community Church. Cute, yes—but he had a super-sized ego to match. Jeri felt the stabbing pain of Rosa's accusation. "I get that you're upset. I would be too. But do you really think *I* would blackmail you?"

Suddenly, Rosa's anger dissolved and she crumpled onto her bed. "No. Not really."

"Let me try to trap her then."

"But what if it goes bad?" She turned a ring around and around on her finger. "No, I'll do what the note says."

Jeri tried another angle. "You said you found the note in your purse. When?"

"In the middle of play practice."

"Before that, when did you last look in your purse?"

Rosa frowned. "Before history class, I think."

"So the note could have been put in there in history class, at supper in the dining hall ..." Jeri ticked off the places on her fingers. "... back here in the dorm, or at the theater during practice."

"That narrows it down to half the school." Rosa rolled her eyes. "Except for during history class, I didn't have my purse with me either." She clenched her fists. "The note could have been stuck in my purse any time in the last five hours."

"And by anyone." Jeri read the note again.

"Anyone who knew about Kevin and me, you mean," Rosa said softly, turning her back.

Jeri's stomach twisted into a painful knot at Rosa's unspoken words. Some part of her still suspected Jeri. That really hurt.

"I don't know how, but I'll nail whoever sent that note," Jeri said. She *had* to find the guilty party—both to save Rosa and to clear her own name. "I'm going on a cookie run. Want one?"

"No." Rosa sniffed. "Thanks anyway."

Five minutes later, Jeri was in the empty lounge eating another sugar cookie when Abby stuck her head in.

"Hey, Jer, want some company?"

Jeri moved over on the love seat to make room. Grateful for a listening ear, she told Abby what had happened.

"That explains why she was so quiet. Usually she's like a tornado blowing through." Abby smiled to soften her words.

Jeri's voice was low. "The hardest part is knowing Rosa doesn't trust me now."

"You're talking rubbish," Abby said.

"Oh yeah? Then how could she say such a thing?"

"She's just scared. You're best chums!"

"Even more reason to trust me! I didn't deserve to be accused like that."

"Can you forgive her?" Abby asked.

Jeri shrugged. "There's nothing to forgive." Jeri pretended it didn't matter to her, but ... what was she supposed to do about her hurt feelings? *I'll catch the blackmailer,* she thought. Then Rosa would feel really guilty for saying that.

On Tuesday morning, Rosa was quiet while they dressed, answering Jeri's questions with one-word answers.

During breakfast, Jeri scouted the dining-hall bathroom for a good hiding place. The ancient restroom had old sinks, clunky pipes, and squeaky faucets. Under the row of sinks, a ruffled skirt of flowered material reached to the floor, hiding the pipes and cleaning products from view.

Jeri pulled back the skirt. It'd be a tight fit, but she'd squeeze in there at noon. She'd arrive early before the students poured in for lunch.

She described her plan to Rosa on the way to science class.

"Just forget it," she replied. "I'm giving her the money. It's the only way to keep her quiet."

"*Please* let me try to catch her first." Jeri paused. "You want to keep your money, don't you?"

Rosa slowly nodded. "Well, yeah ..."

"Okay, then. Leave it to me."

Jeri was on edge all morning, but finally the lunch bell rang. Instead of stopping at the dorm with the others, she headed straight for the dining hall at 11:50. She could hear the cooks talking in the kitchen as she crossed the empty dining hall and slipped into the restroom. She took a sealed white envelope containing cut-up paper and buried it halfway down in the trash. After arranging paper towels over it, she pulled aside the curtain hiding the sink pipes. Down on her hands and knees, she backed in, feet first, and closed the curtain.

She positioned her eye near the seam of the curtain where the opening lined up directly with the trash can. Her nose twitched and her eyes watered from the cleaners' chlorine smell.

As she waited, Jeri tried to imagine who was blackmailing Rosa. It was probably a girl, but it could be a teacher, janitor, or coach. In fact, the janitor could enter the girls' restroom to pick up trash without looking the least bit odd.

A minute later, the noise out in the dining hall exploded as groups of girls arrived. Lunch odors—today's chicken chow mein—blended with the cleaners and made Jeri's empty stomach roll.

Just as Jeri decided to use the curtain to fan the cleaner fumes, the door was pushed open. Holding her breath, she put her eye near the skinny gap. Two girls came in, one heading to the stalls and the other standing at the sink over Jeri's head. Muttering about a soy sauce stain, the girl ran water full blast. It swirled down the pipes near Jeri's head.

Soon they left. Neither had fished around in the trash can. During the next fifteen minutes, Jeri's back began to ache as she counted fourteen girls, from sixth to twelfth grade, come in. Some were alone, some in clumps. The sixth graders were fast—in the stall, flush, wash hands (some), and out the door. Lunch was clearly on their minds.

The high school girls, though, mostly swarmed around the mirror to reapply makeup. They talked nonstop about crush-worthy guys they knew. Once someone kneed Jeri's head but didn't even notice. Rubbing her forehead in annoyance, Jeri wondered if her skull felt like a drain pipe to those boy-crazy dimwits.

Half the time her view of the trash can was obscured by someone at the sink. If anyone fished out the envelope, Jeri didn't see it. A gap of five minutes elapsed when no one came in. By now Jeri's leg had a cramp. She crawled out of her hiding place and dug in the waste can. Rosa's envelope was still there. Thoughtfully, she replaced it and washed her hands.

Again the door opened with a *whoosh*. "Let's go, girls," the Head called out, clapping her hands. "Afternoon classes begin in ten minutes."

Jeri nodded and left, her heart sinking at failing Rosa. The blackmailer must be planning the pickup later. If only it was just a prank or a bad joke!

The dining hall was emptying and the food already put away. *At least the cleaning fumes killed my appetite.* As Jeri passed the bulletin board near the exit, one of the announcements caught her eye.

Are your parents visiting? Bring them to the dining hall for meals. Sign up by Wednesday for the following weekend. Cost of meals will be billed to your student account.

Jeri's stomach churned, and she knew it wasn't entirely from the cleaning fumes. The notice reminded her of her dad's letter. He wanted to come on Friday night and stay through Sunday in a motel in Landmark Hills. So why did she feel mad at the whole idea? She'd dreamed and hoped and prayed for this all year. Yet ... now that he wanted to come, she wished she could avoid him.

She hurried out the exit and down the steps. A hand grabbed her from behind.

"What happened?" Rosa hissed in her ear.

26

"Sheesh! You scared me." Jeri shook her head. "They didn't show. Nothing happened. Sorry."

"*Nada?*" Rosa's jaw went rigid, and she pulled a twenty from her jumper pocket. "Then I'm going back in there before it's too late." She raced up the steps and yanked open the double doors. Headmistress Long blocked her way.

"Where is your destination?" she asked.

"Uh ... I left something in the restroom," Rosa said.

"And that is ...?"

"Um ..."

Head Long arched one eyebrow.

Rosa mumbled, "It's nothing."

"Then you'd best direct yourself to class. Have a good afternoon." And she closed the door.

"Fat chance of that," Rosa muttered, running back down the steps to Jeri. "That blackmailer's gonna find no money and rat on me to the Head about last Sunday. I'm gonna get punished, and it's your fault." She took off running down the sidewalk, head down, dodging among students. She didn't even respond to calls from several girls she passed.

"Hey wait a minute!" Jeri called. *It'll be okay*, she told herself firmly as Rosa disappeared around a corner. They'd talk it out tonight. Rosa would see how wrong she was to blame her.

Jeri had to admit she was scared. It would be her fault if the blackmailer did something awful to Rosa.

Jeri walked to class, barely aware of people rushing around her. All afternoon, her mind jumped around like a jackrabbit. She leaped from worrying about Rosa's black-mailer to what to say to her dad—and back again. Her classes were a blur. Walking back to the dorm later with Abby, she explained about her dad.

"He disappeared out of my life," she said, "and now he's dropping back in, just like that." She snapped her fingers. "Like he expects me to call off my weekend plans."

"What plans?"

"I don't have any, but that's not the point. *He* didn't know that."

Abby was quiet a moment. "What's really bugging you?"

Jeri shuffled along the walk. "I don't deserve how he treated me this year. It isn't fair."

"Well ... who said life was fair?"

"Thanks a lot. I'm not going to lie about how I feel and pretend nothing's wrong."

"You don't have to." Her voice grew very small. "Just remember, you don't always get lots of chances."

Jeri's heart sank. "Abby, I'm sorry. I forgot." Jeri recalled now that Abby's dad had died a couple years ago. She'd probably give anything to spend time with her dad again.

"That's okay," Abby said. "Just think about it. That's all."

Up in her room, Jeri looked up her dad's cell phone number in her address book. It struck her as sad that she couldn't remember it. She was glad for the privacy while Rosa made up her math test.

Leaning against the corner of her desk, she dialed. The call went to voice mail, and her dad's message made her heart beat faster. Mad or not, she liked to hear his voice.

"Dad? I got your letter about coming up. I guess you're still at work. I'll call that number instead."

Without giving herself time to chicken out, Jeri dialed her dad's office. A secretary she didn't know had to transfer the call to another department. *Hmmm.* Had her dad changed jobs this year?

Music played in her ear as she studied the framed photos on her desk. One was taken with her mom on their porch swing; both of them were laughing into the camera and sipping lemonade. The other photo was taken with her dad last August—the last time she'd seen him. They'd gone camping and canoeing on the Yellow River in northeast Iowa. Jeri felt a catch in her throat as she remembered the fun she'd had.

But then he'd met Sabrina and dropped out of Jeri's life.

Her mom, on the other hand, had always been there for her. If only she could talk to her right now. But she was at a business conference in Italy—Jeri hated to bother her unless there was an emergency. Anyway, she knew what Mom would tell her. *Trust God.* From the day Jeri was born, Mom had taught her the meaning of trusting God in the tough times. Her own name—Jeri—even reminded her of that.

Her friends always assumed Jeri was named after her dad. Instead, she was named for the city of Jericho in the

Bible. Her mom's pregnancy had been touch and go, and the doctors wanted her to end it to save her own life. But she'd been determined to carry Jeri as long as possible. For encouragement during the scariest times, she'd clung to certain Bible stories, like when Joshua fought the battle of Jericho. God's plans for Joshua hadn't made sense at all, but Joshua followed God's instructions—and enemy walls just fell down. Trusting God's direction, her mom said, would win the battle every time.

The music stopped. "Mr. McKane is on the line." The professional-sounding voice jerked Jeri out of her thoughts. "Thank you for holding."

"Jeri?" a voice asked. "Is that you?"

"Hi, Dad."

"Did you get my letter?"

"Yesterday." Jeri paused, suddenly tongue-tied.

"How do you feel about having a visitor this weekend?" he finally asked.

"That'd be okay."

The line was silent, except for Dad breathing on the other end.

"Could I come Friday night?" he asked, an edge to his voice.

"Okay."

"I could be there by four thirty. Will you be out of class by then?"

"We get out at three o'clock here." *If you'd been around all year, you'd know that.*

"Then I'll be at your dorm at four thirty. Hampton House, right?"

"Right." Jeri paused, and the words *I love you, Dad* suddenly welled up in her. She took a deep breath, but said "Bye" instead.

"Bye, hon. See you Friday."

Jeri disconnected, glanced again at the photo of her dad, and burst into tears.

After Rosa finished her makeup math exam, she came back to the dorm, but was unusually quiet. Jeri lay on her bed, reading, but watched Rosa out of the corner of her eye.

"Let's go!" Miss Barbara called up the stairs.

"Ready?" Jeri asked, closing her book. The sixth graders were supposed to march two by two to the dining hall, led by the house mother, Ms. Carter, and her assistant, Miss Barbara.

"In a sec." Rosa clicked on another email.

Jeri was waiting in the doorway when Rosa let out a gasp. "What's the matter?" Jeri asked.

"Look at this." Rosa pointed to the screen. "It was sent to the Head too. I'll probably get suspended now." Her voice rose in panic. "I *wanted* to give her the money! I told you this would happen!"

Heart pounding, Jeri leaned over Rosa's shoulder and read:

To Headmistress Long: Last week, Rosa Sanchez skipped church to sneak off to Gracey Park with Kevin Mahoney.

Jeri reached for Rosa, who jerked away. "Look what you've done!"

"I never thought ..." Jeri reread the message. Wait till the headmistress saw that! And then she noticed the sender's address. It was from ULBSawree. *You'll be sorry.*

No kidding.

3
fall-out

"We're leaving!" Ms. Carter called up the stairs. "Jeri? Rosa?"

Without a word, Rosa dashed past Jeri and ran down the stairs. Jeri took a last glance at the email and followed, grabbing her coat off the hall tree as she passed.

As happened every evening, the carillon bells were playing "Now the Day Is Over." Jeri stole frequent glances at Rosa, who stared angrily ahead and said nothing. Jeri trudged silently beside her, surprised that Rosa could be quiet that long. Usually she chattered nonstop, whether anyone was listening or not.

If Rosa wasn't mad, Jeri would have enjoyed the walk tonight. The smell of sun-warmed earth reminded her of planting petunias and impatiens with Mom every spring. Overhead, maples and tulip poplars were budding. Soon cherry trees would bloom, filling the air with heavy perfume.

In the supper line, Rosa silently studied the desserts. Behind her, Jeri noticed Headmistress Long approaching.

"Rosa Sanchez?" Her voice was quiet, yet sharp. "Please come with me."

Rosa whirled around, fear written plainly on her face. She gave Jeri a pleading look that begged, *Come with me!*

Jeri hesitated a moment and then followed Rosa and the headmistress to a corner of the room.

The Head looked quizzically at Jeri. "Your presence is not required here."

"I know." Jeri tried to smile and failed miserably. "Rosa wants me to stay. We're roommates."

"I'm aware of that, but this is a private matter," the Head said. "Please go eat."

Jeri threw Rosa an apologetic glance and left. She watched them from across the room. Rosa merely stood, head hanging, while the Head spoke. In two minutes, Rosa was back in line.

"You okay?" Jeri asked. "What did she say?"

"She asked about the email. She intended to check out the story with Kevin's headmaster. I said she didn't need to, that I did skip church last week with him."

"Did you tell her you got blackmailed?"

"No. What's the point now?" Rosa sighed. "I'm grounded to the campus for a month, and she's also writing a letter to my parents."

"Oh, no!"

"That's not all." Tears welled up in her eyes. "I have to drop out of *Cinderella*."

"No way! Doesn't she know you're the star?"

"Not anymore."

"This is nuts! Opening night is only ten days away."

"I know." Her voice dropped to a whisper. "Twenty measly bucks wasn't worth all this."

Prodded from behind, Jeri moved past the rolls and butter and got her milk. "I was only trying to help. And it doesn't matter that it was only twenty dollars. You shouldn't have to pay twenty dollars for privacy."

"Well, hot-shot detective, I'm paying a bigger price now!"

"I really *am* sorry about that. But even if I had extra cash, I'd never hand it over to some cruddy blackmailer."

"Easy for you to say." Rosa shook her head. "I should have handled it myself."

Jeri followed Rosa to their table. If only she could undo some of the damage. *Maybe* ... "I'll be right back." She set down her tray of food, straightened her shoulders, and marched over to the Head's corner of the room. With two other ladies, she shared a small elegant table, complete with fresh-cut flowers. Jeri cleared her throat. "Excuse me."

"Yes?" The Head wiped her lips on a linen napkin.

"Could I talk to you? Please?" Jeri was appalled that her voice—along with her knees—shook.

"Go ahead." She glanced at her co-workers. "They won't mind."

I do, though. The last thing she needed was an audience.

"Yes?" Headmistress Long asked again. "I would like to finish my meal while it's warm."

"Um, I just wanted to say that Rosa is really sorry about going to the park with Kevin. I know she won't do it again."

"She told me the same thing."

"Well, you can believe her."

"That's good to know." A slight smile played on her lips. "Is that all?"

Jeri took a deep breath. "I know her punishment isn't my business, but ..." Her voice trailed off. Would this get *her* grounded?

The headmistress sat very still, saying nothing, and the other ladies stopped eating. Jeri cleared her throat again. "It seems to me that grounding her for a month and telling her parents is enough. Having to quit the play is too much. Especially with it being so close."

The Head leaned forward. "You don't understand the seriousness of deception. Claiming to attend church when you plan to meet a boy breaks several rules Landmark girls are expected to obey."

"But Rosa didn't do that."

"She most assuredly did."

"No, I mean she didn't plan it. She *did* plan to go to church Sunday. Kevin's in our Sunday school class. Remember how warm it was that day? Just for fun, they decided to leave and see if the creek was thawing."

"Are you sure of your information?"

"Positive."

The Head glanced at the other ladies, and an unspoken message seemed to pass among them. Then she said, "What Rosa did was still very wrong, even if it was spur of the moment."

Jeri cocked her head to one side. Did she hear a "but" in there?

"But I can understand how it happened. I feel like playing hooky on these warm days myself."

Jeri was almost afraid to ask. "Do you mean ...?"

The Head nodded. "This time I agree with you. Grounding and notifying her parents is enough." The other ladies smiled and nodded. "Tell Rosa she can be Cinderella next weekend after all."

"Yes!" Jeri's right arm shot into the air. "Thank you, Ms. Long."

When Jeri gave Rosa the news, Rosa squealed and gave her a quick hug. *Now maybe she'll believe I had nothing to do with that blackmail note.* After supper, Rosa headed to practice with a skip in her step. Grinning, Jeri continued on to the dorm to work on their media project, relieved that the crisis was past.

There Jeri spread her work out on her bed, glad to concentrate on putting together their little newspaper. It had started as a group assignment for herself, Rosa, Abby, and Nikki. It had been a hit with their friends—especially Rosa's advice column—so they'd decided to keep publishing a two-page weekly paper.

Tonight she'd edit her *Cinderella* article. Then she'd work on Abby's article, "Knockout Room Redo's," about transforming drab dorm rooms to sleek and swanky. Abby's articles rocked, but Jeri usually had to fix spots that were British-sounding and confusing: words with extra *u*'s like *favour* or where Abby used *pound* for dollar or *mate* for friend.

Although Jeri loved producing their little paper, she secretly hoped to be the first sixth-grade reporter for Landmark School's *Lightning Bolt*. Her chances were slim, but the next morning she planned to show the newspaper's advisor her media project. Just in case.

On Wednesday morning Jeri stopped by Herald Hall on the way to her first class. She paused outside the newspaper office, prayed for courage, and pushed open the door. The office had a high counter running the length of it, keeping visitors from invading the busy press room behind. Jeri stood in awe, yearning to push through the little swinging door at the end of the counter.

A girl with tiny glasses stepped forward from her desk. "Need something?"

"Can I, uh, see the person in charge of the paper?"

"You mean the editor?" the girl asked.

"I guess so."

"She's not here." The girl smirked.

"Then who's in charge?"

"That's me, Claire. Junior editor." She wiped her smudged glasses on her shirttail. "You want to sell papers for us?"

"Not exactly." Jeri laid her manila envelope on the counter. "I want to write for the paper."

The junior editor grinned. "Oh sure ... like in a few years."

Jeri sighed. "Do you ever let sixth graders do *any* kind of writing for the paper?"

"Not a chance," Claire said. "Sixth graders can't write. Not good enough. You're just a kid."

Jeri bristled at that. "How old are *you*?"

"Ninth grade."

"Oh. Well, *I* can write." She pushed the envelope across the counter. "Here are some samples."

"Of what? Your little English assignments? 'What I Did on My Summer Vacation'?"

"No, they're editions of a newspaper that three of my friends and I put out." Jeri felt the heat crawling up her neck to her cheeks. "I use Publisher software."

Claire rolled her eyes. "I'm sure they're—"

"'Morning, Claire." A teacher came in and went behind the counter. "How's it going this morning?"

Suddenly Claire was all business. "Johanna's late. She had to retake those photos. Unless Rachel's debate article is here by ten, I'll need something else for front page." She grinned maliciously then. "And this sixth grader wants to be a cub reporter." She tapped Jeri's manila envelope. "Don't worry. I told her we're not hiring kids."

The teacher picked up the envelope, and Jeri's heart beat triple-time. "I'm Mrs. Gludell. I oversee things here. And you are ...?"

"Jeri McKane."

"Well, Jeri, let's see what you brought."

Jeri caught Claire's piercing glare. "I'll be working if you need me," Claire said.

Mrs. Gludell spread Jeri's sheets of paper on the counter. Without comment or expression, she read each edition. Jeri had also included her new article about the musical. Finally Mrs. Gludell removed her glasses and looked up. "Is this your work?" she asked. "100 percent?"

"The musical article is. And these articles." She pointed to the ones she'd written. "I also put together our little newspaper on my computer." Jeri bit her bottom lip.

"They're very good. You have a good sense of journalistic integrity."

Over the teacher's shoulder, Jeri spotted Claire listening— and scowling. Jeri didn't care now. *I have journalistic integrity?* That sounded cool, even if she didn't know what it meant. "Thank you."

"Can I keep these for a while?" Mrs. Gludell asked. "Do you have copies?"

Jeri nodded. "I always back up everything."

The teacher grinned. "One of our first rules!" She put the papers back into the envelope. "I'm especially interested in the article on the musical."

Claire hurried forward then. "Actually, Mrs. Gludell, I'm working on a piece about the play myself. I've got some great behind-the-scenes stuff."

"Excellent. Show me when you're done." She glanced at her watch. "I'd better run, or I'll be late to class." The teacher slipped out from behind the counter. "Thanks for stopping by, Jeri. We always need new talent." She left, and Jeri was about to follow when she heard a *hiss* behind her.

"Don't get a big head," Claire said. "Mrs. Gludell says that to everyone. She's only being nice. You won't hear from her."

Without comment, Jeri left the newspaper office. What did that Claire know anyway? She was just a kid too. Still, Jeri had a sinking feeling Claire was probably telling the truth—*this* time.

At the end of the day, an office monitor arrived in Jeri's biology class with a message. "You're wanted in the newspaper office right after school."

Jeri nodded, her mind jumping from one hopeful idea to another. Maybe the advisor wanted another reporter. Maybe she thought Claire needed an assistant. Or ... maybe Claire wanted to return her envelope ... with a sneering "Told you so."

Well, she'd know soon. She headed across the open courtyard to Herald Hall, her high hopes warring against her common sense.

In the newspaper office, Mrs. Gludell worked at a huge desk behind the counter. "Come on back," she called.

Jeri felt a thrill as she pushed through the swinging door. "I got your note," she said, holding it out.

"I've read your material several times." Mrs. Gludell tapped a fingernail on the article about the musical. "Unless you have other plans for this piece, I'd like to run it in the *Lightning Bolt*. Front page."

"You're kidding!"

The teacher laughed. "I'm serious. We had an unexpected delay with another article. I love your piece, although it's wordy and needs editing."

Jeri blinked. It needed editing? She didn't think it was wordy at all. There was a lot more she could have said. Still ... front page! And most of it was about Rosa—that would make her head spin.

"Would my article be in *this* Friday's paper?" Jeri asked. Mrs. Gludell nodded. Jeri's dad was coming Friday. She'd buy an extra copy to give him!

"Next week," the teacher added, "come talk to me about where we can best use your talents."

"Really?"

"Welcome to the team."

Jeri almost floated out of the newspaper office. Now she understood what people meant by walking on air.

Out in the hall, Claire rushed around a corner and plowed into her. "Well, if it isn't the little hot-shot reporter." She tossed her long red hair over her shoulder. "Just remember: *I'm* the editor. You'll work for me." She laughed. "Or not."

4
strike two

At supper Wednesday night Jeri told her friends about getting an article in the *Lightning Bolt*. "The best part is giving Rosa free publicity."

"Smashing! Let's hear it for Rosa!" Abby clinked her fork against her water glass. Nikki whistled and swung her arm in a circle over her head, as if she were roping a steer.

Rosa grinned, stood, and took a bow. "If you hadn't talked to the Head, I wouldn't even *be* in the play. I owe ya, Jeri."

Jeri's face grew warm, and she bent over her chicken and rice, thankful that things were right with Rosa again.

Abby reached across the table and grabbed Jeri's arm. "This calls for a party! Come over and we'll get pizza and a movie—"

"Abby!" Jeri said, laughing. "That sounds awesome, but that stuff costs money. You're as broke as I am."

"Mum sent me a couple tenners a while ago, and I saved 'em for a special occasion." Abby studied their puzzled expressions. "Sorry. Ten pounds. Ten quid?" Then she grinned. "Sorry, mates. Ten dollar bills."

"I wish my mom would send *me* a few tenners," Jeri said.

"Mum said she wishes she could meet all of you." Abby sighed.

"I hear you." Rosa stirred salsa into her rice. "It's hard when they're halfway around the world—mine in Chile, yours in England."

"I forget what your mom does," Nikki said.

"She's a curator at the Jane Austen Centre in Bath. It's a museum about a famous English writer."

"What's a curator?" Rosa asked, laying a hand against her forehead. "Does she cure the sick?"

Abby laughed. "It just means she's in charge of running the museum. Lots of Jane Austen books are made into movies, so she meets the actors and actresses some-times. Mostly she arranges tours." She sipped her soda. "Other books *about* Jane Austen are sold there too, and Mum makes sure people don't steal them."

Jeri frowned. "She's a cop too?"

"Not steal that way. She keeps them from being copied without permission. It's against the law." She tucked her hair behind her ears. "Anyway, Mum got a raise and sent me some spending money. Sure you don't want to celebrate with a party?"

"Nah. You keep your money," Jeri said. "But thanks anyway."

"Okay." She glanced at her watch and pushed back her chair. "I'm going back early. Mum said she'd try to call tonight."

The other girls went back to the dorm soon after. Jeri needed to write a different article for their weekly paper since Mrs. Gludell was using the one about the musical. She followed her roommate upstairs. "Hey, could I have your 'Dear Rosa' column before you go to practice?"

"Okay, as soon as I add one more question," Rosa said.

When they opened their door, Jeri's foot crunched on a piece of paper. She'd stepped on a note slipped under their door. Scrawled on the outside was "Dear Rosa."

"Looks like the question you needed," Jeri said, handing it over. She opened her Publisher program and found the file she needed. A gasp behind her made her whirl around.

Rosa held the note with the tips of her fingers, as if it might burn her. Panic filled her eyes. "Check this out."

Jeri took the note and read aloud: "I know your dad isn't your dad. Your mom wasn't married when she had you. Pay $100, or your secret will be public. Leave the money in locker 14 after gym class Friday. No tricks this time!"

"A hundred dollars!" Jeri exclaimed.

Rosa snatched the note back. "Is that all you can say?" she wailed. "This is horrible! How did anyone find out about Mom?"

"You're right. It's horrible. But don't pay her, Rosa."

"Really? Look what happened the last time!"

"But if you do, the price will keep going up. It's always like that in detective stories." Jeri hesitated. "Don't be embarrassed. Even if people found out about your mom, I really don't think they'd care."

Rosa chewed her lower lip. "I don't embarrass that easily." She gazed at the family picture on her desk.

"Then why even *consider* paying a hundred dollars?"

"Because of the missionary board," Rosa said.

"Why? They'd already know about your family, right?"

"They might know that my brothers are from Mom's first marriage, and that her first husband died." She picked up the photo. "I bet they don't know I was born six years before she married Dad."

"What would happen if they found out?"

"I don't know. Missionary boards are strict. You have to report to them every month about how your family is doing, any problems you're having ... If this blackmail thing about Mom became public, my parents might have to leave Chile. It could ruin them!"

"I think your imagination's gone crazy," Jeri said. "I really doubt that would happen."

"But I can't take that chance!"

Silence fell heavily on the room. "Well, we have till Friday," Jeri finally said. "I'll work on this."

"Like you worked on the other blackmail note?" Rosa asked. "No way. I'm paying the money."

"Oh sure. Where are you gonna get a hundred bucks?"

Rosa wrapped her arms tightly around herself. "I don't know. But my family is too important to take chances."

"I wonder how she found out about your mom, anyway."

Rosa's voice was soft as a whisper. *"You're* the only one I told about Dad adopting me."

"But I kept your secret! I never even told Mom."

Rosa was silent, but her breathing was raspy.

"Are you *sure* you didn't tell anyone else besides me?"

"Positive." Rosa glanced at the clock. "I have to go, or I'll be late for practice."

Eyes averted, Rosa grabbed her music folder and left. Jeri sank into her desk chair, stunned that it had happened again. She'd just gotten Rosa's trust back, and now this. Jeri couldn't blame her for wondering, but it really hurt just the same. Rosa should know—

The phone interrupted her thoughts, and she grabbed it. "Jeri? It's Miss Kimberly."

"Rosa just left."

"Actually, I wanted to talk to you. Can you come to practice?"

"Now? I guess. Why?"

Miss Kimberly yawned loudly into the phone. "Mrs. Gludell showed me your article—the one for Friday's paper. It's excellent! I wondered if you'd do some more publicity before opening night."

"Really?" Jeri did some quick thinking. Having a reason to hang out at the theater would help her keep an eye on Rosa—and watch for a blackmailer. "Sure, I'd like to. I have to ask Ms. Carter first."

"I'll call her right now," Miss Kimberly said. "Oh, by the way, I heard that Rosa was suspended from the play, and that you asked Headmistress Long to let her finish. Thank you!" She yelled some stage directions to someone in the background. "See you soon."

Jeri arrived when Esmerelda and Prunella were singing "Stepsisters' Lament." She had to admit that Britney's facial expressions and outlandish actions were really funny. Britney totally outshone Hailey onstage—and if Rosa didn't perk up, Esmerelda would outshine Cinderella too.

Jeri craned her neck but didn't spot Rosa anywhere. She was probably backstage practicing her lines—or worrying herself sick over that second blackmail note.

During a break while the stage hands changed the scenery, Miss Kimberly joined Jeri in the front row. She tried to wedge herself into a seat. Jeri looked away in embarrassment, hoping she didn't get stuck. "Thanks for giving your time to promote the play," Miss Kimberly said breathlessly. She squirmed a bit, lowering one hip in the seat. "I thought you might do short write-ups of each character in the play. I could get photos if you don't have a camera."

"I'll check out a digital one at the media center," Jeri said, looking at the floor and the stage—anywhere but where Miss Kimberly sat sideways, one hip filling the chair as she leaned on an armrest.

"Could you write a short history of this theater? There are fascinating stories about it."

"Where would I find those?" Jeri asked doubtfully.

"Books and pamphlets in the library." She shifted again, hoisted herself to her feet, and rubbed her hip. "Some students will be playing songs from the musical on the clock tower's carillon too. You could put that in your article. Britney, Lara, and Lisa will take turns."

Jeri scribbled her ideas in a notebook. Miss Kimberly arched her back and rubbed it. Then she massaged her temples with tiny circular motions.

"You okay?" Jeri asked.

"Sometimes I get these wretched headaches—so bad it blurs my vision. Pinched nerves."

Just then, Rosa appeared at the edge of the stage. "I tried on the ball gown like you asked."

"Good. Does it fit?"

"No! I can practically swim in it. They let out every extra bit of material in the seams." She rolled her eyes. "I'm not *that* big!"

"Of course not," Miss Kimberley said. "The seamstress must have misunderstood. I'll take it back. There's plenty of time." She stared at Rosa. "Is there something else? You look upset."

Rosa shot Jeri a warning glance. "I'm just nervous about the play starting soon."

Miss Kimberly nodded and then frowned, as if the small head movement was painful. "Most leading ladies have opening night jitters, but end up doing a great job. I starred in some plays back in college, and I understand what you're going through. You'll be terrific!"

Jeri agreed that Rosa would be terrific, but Miss Kimberly definitely did *not* know what Rosa was going through.

Miss Kimberly climbed up the steps—with several pauses to catch her breath—and disappeared backstage. Then Rosa said, "That dress is so big even Miss Kimberly could wear it." And she stomped off herself.

Jeri glanced around, wondering what to do first. Since she already had Britney's "before" and "after" photos, she might as well start by interviewing Miss Bubbly. She stepped behind the curtain and picked her way around swords, crowns, plates of artificial food, and costumes hanging on changing screens. She heard Britney's high-pitched voice before she spotted her. The words she heard made her pull back behind the papier-mâché horse and pumpkin coach.

"Come on. I know you have it," Britney said in a wheedling tone.

"You're wrong. I don't have fifty bucks."

Jeri closed her eyes to concentrate. That sounded like Lisa, a stagehand.

"Don't your parents send you money?" Britney demanded.

"I have a debit card, and they put money in the account."

"Even better! I'll pay you back in a couple weeks."

"It's not that easy," the other girl said. "Dad watches my account online like a hawk. Every time I buy something, I get a call. If I took out fifty dollars, he'd be on the phone before I left the bank."

"Well *fine*," Britney said. "See if I ever help you!"

Jeri stayed behind the pumpkin until Britney charged by. A moment later, Lisa went to move some scenery into place. Jeri thought about what she'd just overheard. So Britney was short of money ... Was she desperate enough to try blackmail? Jeri knew Britney had wanted to be Cinderella. If the Head hadn't changed her mind, Rosa's role would be vacant now. Was Britney still hoping to step into Rosa's glass slippers?

Miss Kimberly called Rosa and Hilary Lyttle, a ninth grader, to center stage. Their two duets, "Impossible" and "It's Possible," were next. Jeri spotted Lisa talking to Hailey and worked her way toward them. She nearly tripped over a box of makeup and grease paint, and she wondered again how anyone survived a play without fractured bones. Maybe *this* was the real reason theater people told each other to "break a leg."

Lisa and Hailey watched Rosa move into the spotlight for her song. Then Jeri overheard something that made her shrink back into the shadows.

Lisa snickered. "Can you believe they cast a sixth grader as the star?"

Hailey made a gagging sound. "My 'rents are gonna have a cow." She lowered her voice to a gravelly pitch. " 'I don't send you to an expensive boarding school to have it overrun with Mexicans!' "

Jeri stifled a gasp. What was *that* supposed to mean?

Lisa said, "We ought to send *that* Mexican south of the border. Cinderella's supposed to have blue eyes and blonde hair. I mean *really*, what were they thinking?"

Jeri clenched her fists, wishing she could jump out and smack those girls. If she didn't need to eavesdrop on possible suspects, she'd give them a piece of her mind. Didn't any of the older girls like Rosa?

When practice was over, Rosa walked home with Jeri, but she barely said five words. Jeri sighed. Were they back to Rosa not trusting her again?

Coming around the corner of the building, she was hit by a blast of cold wind that cut through her jacket. The weather was so unpredictable lately. Hopefully it'd warm up over the weekend so she could do some stuff outside with her dad. Maybe he'd like to go for a horseback ride. He'd be so impressed that she'd learned to ride.

Before then, though, she needed some answers from Rosa. "What do you know about Lisa and Hailey?" she asked.

Rosa kept walking. "Nothing much. They don't talk to me a whole lot. Why?"

"I'm doing some publicity about everyone in the play," she said. "What do you think about them?"

Rosa shrugged. "They're okay, I guess."

"Are they nice to you?"

"Not since Hailey said I stole her boyfriend." Rosa laughed. "I couldn't help that he hung around me at the Christmas dance." She stopped and faced Jeri. "You don't need that for any article. What's up?"

"The blackmail notes—they're obviously being sent by someone who doesn't like you." She wouldn't repeat the horrible things she'd overheard, but maybe the girls had said or done other things to Rosa.

"I don't really know either girl," Rosa said. "The upper classmen either pick on us lowly sixth graders or they ignore us. Usually I'm too busy having fun to notice them either. Until now, that is."

Jeri didn't argue as they turned the corner to Hampton House, but someone *was* noticing Rosa—and hating her enough to blackmail her. She got the first note at practice, which suggested it was someone in the play. And the second blackmail note had been delivered to their dorm room. Was the blackmailer from Hampton House?

"What other sixth graders are in the play?" Jeri asked. She'd only seen part of the cast at practice. Miss Kimberly said the first full rehearsal wasn't until Monday.

"I'm the only sixth grader with a speaking part." Rosa

paused on the front steps of the dorm. "Abby plays in the orchestra though. They've been practicing in the band room so far." She opened the door, and light from the hall spilled outside. "The orchestra starts practicing with us next week. No more taped music. Yea!"

Rosa hurried inside, but Jeri was frozen in place. *Abby?*

She'd forgotten that Abby was playing her flute in the musical. Suddenly other memories crowded her mind. Abby had wanted to order pizza and rent movies; did her money come from England ... or from blackmail? And she'd been in Sunday school, so *she'd* seen Rosa leave with Kevin. And *she* could have delivered the second blackmail note unseen—she'd gone back to the dorm early, supposedly for a phone call from her mom. Since Abby's room was next to theirs, eavesdropping about Rosa's mom would have been a snap.

Shivering, Jeri jammed her hands in her coat pockets. It was all what the police called circumstantial evidence. It didn't necessarily mean anything.

Or did it?

5
keeping secrets

"Pass the honey, please," Jeri said, spreading real butter on her baking powder biscuits.

The house mother and her assistant had outdone themselves this Thursday morning, fixing biscuits and muffins, sausage gravy, and fried potatoes. Twice a week, the girls ate breakfast in their dorms instead of trudging through the cold to the dining hall. Jeri loved it. They could eat in their pajamas instead of dressed in their uniforms.

It almost felt like home, she thought.

"Where's Rosa?" Ms. Carter asked.

"Still in the shower." Jeri drizzled honey on her biscuits. "Want me to get her before it's all gone?"

Ms. Carter laughed. "There's plenty. She's smart, showering before the hot water runs out. In fact, I bet—"

"Hey, you!" screamed someone upstairs. "Help, some-body!" A door slammed hard.

Jeri nearly choked on her biscuit. Ms. Carter charged up the steps with five girls right behind her. Above, someone continued to yell for help. At the top of the stairs, they turned to the east wing. Mariah Lounsberry, in her bathrobe with her hair up in a towel, hung on to the knob of her bedroom door.

"Ms. Carter, hurry!" Mariah called. "I've got a robber trapped in there!" She flung open the door. "Look!"

Jeri peered over the house mother's shoulder. She couldn't believe her eyes. The girl slouched on Mariah's bed was Rosa!

Ms. Carter cocked her head to one side. "Rosa? What are you doing?"

"Looks obvious to me," Mariah cried. "She was ripping me off while I took a shower!"

The teacher patted her shoulder. "Go back into the bathroom and dry your hair. You other girls finish your breakfast. We'll straighten out this misunderstanding."

Although the other girls went downstairs, Jeri hung back in the doorway. She knew what Rosa was doing. *This* was her plan to dig up the hundred dollars!

Ms. Carter sat down on the edge of the bed and put a hand under Rosa's chin. "Look at me, dear," the house mother said. "What are you doing with her purse?"

"Nothing."

The house mother waited, watching Rosa. "Did

Mariah take something of yours? Or were you borrowing something?"

Rosa shook her head.

"This isn't like you," Ms. Carter said.

Jeri stepped forward then. "Rosa, tell her what's wrong."

"Jeri, be quiet! I mean it!"

Ms. Carter frowned. "What's going on, girls? I can't help with a problem if I don't know what it is."

Rosa glared at Jeri, silently warning her to keep the secret. Jeri felt ripped in two. She couldn't betray Rosa's trust, but if someone didn't explain ...

Rosa hung her head. "I was thinking about taking Mariah's money, but I didn't." She handed the purse to Ms. Carter.

"But why would you steal from Mariah—or anyone?" the house mother asked.

"Rosa! Tell her!"

Rosa stared at the floor, refusing to meet the house mother's gaze. Ms. Carter looked at Jeri, who hung her head. It wasn't her secret to tell. Rosa would rather have people believe she was a thief than have them think badly of her mom.

Ms. Carter's voice was sad. "Go to your room now, Rosa. I'll be there to talk to you in a few minutes."

As soon as they were back in their room, Jeri said, "You've got to tell—"

"No! Now leave me alone!"

Jeri waited, then shrugged and went to take her

shower. When she came back, Ms. Carter was there. "I know what you said, but you were found in her room with her purse. Mariah claims she had thirty dollars in her wallet. There's only twenty in there now." She waited, but there was only silence. "I have to report this to the head-mistress immediately. Prepare yourself. She has a zero-tolerance policy for theft." She pulled Rosa to her feet. "We live together like a family, and a family needs trust."

"I understand, but I didn't take the money." Rosa's voice was small and defeated. "You can search me if you want."

"I'm afraid that wouldn't help now."

Jeri stood unmoving in the doorway. If only Ms. Carter had searched Rosa while she was still in Mariah's room. Now Mariah could say Rosa had hidden the stolen money while Jeri was in the shower.

After Rosa left with the house mother, Jeri got ready for school. *Surely nothing really bad would happen to Rosa. After all, she hadn't actually taken any money*—Jeri believed that. After her first period class, she ran into Mariah in the restroom.

"Did you hear the teachers in the hall?" she asked smugly. "Rosa got expelled."

Jeri's heart nearly stopped. "What! She's leaving Landmark?"

"Don't act so shocked. What did you think would happen to the little thief?"

"Rosa never took your money!"

"Get real! You think it's a coincidence that I'm missing ten dollars right after I find Rosa in my room with my purse?"

Jeri bit back nasty words. "When is she leaving?"

"I don't know ..." Mariah ran off to tell another girl the news.

The rest of the morning was a nightmare, and Jeri sat through her classes in a daze. Would Rosa be gone by tonight? Would Dad even get to meet her best friend? If Rosa left before the blackmailer was caught, she'd never know for sure that it wasn't Jeri. Maybe Mariah was wrong about what she'd heard. Hope surged, followed quickly by grim reality. Rosa had been caught red-handed. No begging on Jeri's part would get her off the hook this time.

Skipping lunch, Jeri raced back to Hampton House. When she burst into their room, Rosa was there— packing. "You really have to leave? Didn't the Head believe you? You didn't take any money!"

Rosa sniffled. "Not according to Mariah. She said ten bucks was missing." She pulled books and clothes from her closet to pack into several large cardboard boxes on the bed.

"This is so wrong!" Jeri said. "When do you go?"

"Sunday night. My aunt and uncle are driving from Arizona to get me."

"*Please* tell the Head about the blackmail notes! You're just trying to protect your mom. She might understand better than you think."

"I'm not telling, and you can't either. You *promised*!"

Jeri sighed. "You know I won't." *But you can't stop me from trying to trap the blackmailer before Sunday, with or without your help*, she thought.

Rosa sat beside Jeri on her bed. "You're my best friend, and I was thinking while I packed. I don't know how the blackmailer found out about my mom, but I know you didn't tell anyone. I trust you."

"Thanks. I hoped you'd believe me." *And you really should have all along*, she didn't say out loud.

Rosa sighed deeply. "I can't believe I go on Sunday."

"Over my dead body," Jeri mumbled. "Can I at least have the blackmail note? I won't show anyone, but maybe I can pick up a clue from it."

"I guess." Rosa took the note out from under her pillow.

"You should come to classes the rest of the week," Jeri said, slipping the note inside a book. "Cuz then if I—no, when I—catch the blackmailer, you won't have a lot of classes to make up."

"Yeah, right. I think I'll pack instead," Rosa said. "Then I have to return my play script to Miss Kimberly."

Jeri stood and watched helplessly. *Lord, what should I do? You know who the blackmailer is. Please show me—and in time to keep Rosa from being expelled.*

What would she ever do without Rosa? They'd been through so much together. She wanted to spend every minute with her now. Of all weekends for Dad to show up!

Jeri put her arm around Rosa's shoulders and squeezed. Rosa might not have any faith in her—Jeri didn't have much faith in herself either—but she had a *ton* of faith in God. He hadn't let her down yet, and he wouldn't now.

6

the spy

Jeri raced back across campus to the dining hall at the end of lunch period. She barely noticed the aroma of peach cobbler, despite her missed lunch. She was on a mission—and success was critical.

She made a beeline for Miss Kimberly's table, where the young director ate alone. "Can I talk to you a minute?" Jeri asked, breathless.

Miss Kimberly swallowed her last heaping forkful. "Don't tell me you've written those publicity articles already!"

"No, it's something more important." She leaned closer. "Did you know Rosa is packing to leave school this weekend?"

"*What?* What do you mean, leaving? Before the play? She can't!"

Jeri felt a surge of hope. "It might be up to you to change that. She got expelled today. Her aunt and uncle are coming to get her on Sunday."

"Expelled? Rosa? I can't believe it!" She frowned. "I had a message earlier to call the headmistress. This must be why."

"Could you call her now and ask her to change her mind?"

"No, I'll see her personally. If Rosa leaves, we lose our star." Miss Kimberly thought for a moment. "This spring musical pulls in half the town and tons of parents. It's a big moneymaker for the school. The headmistress knows that. We need our star performer!"

"What if she doesn't listen?"

"Then *I* might have to play Cinderella!" Miss Kimberly said with a wink.

Jeri laughed, glad the director had a sense of humor. She could just imagine mammoth Miss Kimberly waltzing around with Prince Charming.

Miss Kimberly tossed two white pills into her mouth, gulped from her glass of water, and swallowed. *Another headache?* Jeri wondered. "I'll go now," Miss Kimberly said, gripping the table's edge and heaving herself to her feet. "Rosa's not a troublemaker. A fun-loving chatterbox, yes, but good-hearted."

Jeri agreed 100 percent. "Can I go with you to see the headmistress?"

Miss Kimberly ran a hand through her short curls. "I guess so. I'll write you a pass for your next class."

"Thank you!"

The headmistress was available, but the meeting was brief. "No exceptions, even for the play," she said firmly. "Mariah's money is missing, and witnesses saw Rosa in Mariah's room with her purse. Stealing is never acceptable among Landmark girls."

Jeri couldn't believe what was happening. Outside, she stared around the deserted campus. "Thanks for trying, Miss Kimberly."

"I wish—for all our sakes—that I could have done more."

"Who will replace Rosa?"

"Her understudy. A seventh grader named Sarah James."

"Rosa never told me about any understudy."

"Really? We always have one. I imagine she never expected to need her."

Jeri frowned, trying to remember. "I never saw this Sarah at rehearsals."

"She's been sick all week—just a flu bug." The director dug in her purse for a pen to write Jeri a tardy excuse.

An understudy? Of course! Which actress had the best motive for getting rid of Rosa? The girl ready to take over the lead. She must know all the speeches and songs by now. A few blackmail notes and voilà! Sarah's the new star.

When Miss Kimberly gave Jeri the note, her hand had a slight tremor. "Sarah's voice has improved since last year. She takes private lessons, but I wonder if she can pull it off. She doesn't have Rosa's … flair. Actually, Rosa reminds me of myself at her age." She smiled as if to herself and headed off toward the theater.

After stopping to check out a digital camera, Jeri hurried to literature class, wishing she had a magic way to turn back the clock.

Rosa wouldn't go to the dining hall for supper, preferring soup alone in the dorm kitchen to facing the whole school. "You go ahead," she told Jeri. "I'm okay."

"If you're sure." Jeri took a deep breath. "I still have to go to play practice after supper. Miss Kimberly asked me to write some more short articles." But she intended to spend most of her energy finding Rosa's blackmailer.

"I really let everyone down." Rosa hesitated. "Is Miss Kimberly mad at me?"

"No, but she doesn't think Sarah James is half as good as you either."

"Good." Rosa grinned, but then her smile faded. "Just kidding. I really do want the musical to be awesome."

Later, on the way to rehearsal, Jeri reviewed her list of suspects. First was Britney. She'd wanted the starring role, she had access to Rosa's purse at the theater, she was short on cash, and—while nice to Rosa's face—she backstabbed her with her friends. Then there was the understudy. How much did Sarah want the starring role?

She'd had to learn all the songs and speeches. That was tons of work for nothing. Had she taken steps to eliminate Rosa? Or were Hailey and Lisa working together? Were they so jealous of Rosa they'd try to get rid of her? Jeri could believe it.

And then ... there was Abby. Jeri forced herself to look at the facts. Abby had the easiest access to Rosa—her purse and her secrets. She had extra money to spend lately. And she was the only suspect—Jeri winced at thinking of her like that—who could have slipped the note under their door without arousing suspicion.

But how could Abby be the blackmailer? She was so kind and sweet. And why? Just for a chance to switch room-mates? Abby wasn't best friends with Nikki, but she'd never go that far to room with Jeri. No, it just couldn't be Abby.

When Jeri arrived at the theater, she hung her coat on a hook by the back door, grabbed her notebook and pen, and waited in the wings to interview Salli. The "prince" was onstage singing "Ten Minutes Ago I Saw You." Earlier in the week, Rosa had been the other half of the duet. The petite prince now sang to Miss Kimberly instead—and they looked ridiculous. Where was the understudy? Still sick? When her song was over, Salli was so eager to talk that Jeri finished the interview in record time.

Then Jeri followed Miss Kimberly to the dressing room to ask about the understudy. If she was still sick, maybe Miss Kimberly could pressure the Head to let Rosa perform after all. Jeri opened the door of the dressing room, but her words died in her throat. Something was wrong. Terribly wrong.

Sitting on the wicker couch, leaning way back, Miss Kimberly gripped the armrest as if she might crush it. In her other hand was a piece of pink paper. Her lips moved as she read it. Various emotions flashed across her face: astonishment, anger, fear, confusion.

She's being blackmailed too! Jeri's heart pounded as she softly closed the door. Now what? Should she ask about it? Of course, it might only be a letter from a friend. Maybe someone was sick or dying. It wouldn't have to be a blackmail note.

Jeri felt the floorboards shake before she heard Miss Kimberly's heavy footsteps. She scooted around the corner out of sight. The director emerged from the dressing room, spewing a string of angry words. Jeri frowned. Was she arguing with herself? When Miss Kimberly brushed against Cinderella's coach, a paper fell from her pocket.

Jeri waited until Miss Kimberly descended, step by slow step, to the orchestra pit. Then she snatched up the note and disappeared into the dressing room. Her back against the door, she unfolded and read: "You have no right to photocopy sheet music. If I tell the company, they will press charges. Leave $150 inside the pumpkin coach on Friday morning before breakfast."

Jeri let out the breath she'd been holding. This *was* a blackmail note. More and more, evidence pointed to a member of *Cinderella* as the blackmailer. Who else would know Miss Kimberly copied music for the cast members?

Jeri gasped. *Abby!*

Miss Kimberly probably photocopied music for the orchestra too. And Abby knew about copyrights because of her mom. Just the day before she'd explained how her mom had to protect people's books from being copied without permission. Jeri felt sick to her stomach. Abby just couldn't be writing these notes. She was so *nice* to everyone!

No, surely it was Britney. Being beaten out of the star role by a mere sixth grader must've really irritated her. Blackmailing the director could be her revenge for choosing Rosa instead of her.

She carefully folded the note. When she got back to the dorm, she'd compare it to Rosa's second blackmail note, the handwritten one. Maybe there was a clue in the paper or the ink, the word choices or spelling—anything!

During the rest of rehearsal, Jeri could barely concentrate. By eight fifteen, when the prince was singing "Do I Love You Because You're Beautiful?" she decided to leave. She picked her way around the props backstage to where she'd hung her coat. She came around a painted partition, but stopped cold and pulled back. Then she peered around it.

Britney was moving slowly down the row, as if hunting for a particular coat. She reached for a pink fleece jacket— Jeri thought it was Lisa's—and slipped a small envelope into the pocket.

At last. Caught in the act.

"Miss Kimberly!" Jeri shouted. "Quick, come here!"

Britney whirled around and dropped the envelope on the floor. Jeri dashed forward, stooped, and grabbed it.

"Give that back!" Britney demanded.

"No way," Jeri said, breathing hard. "Face it, Britney. It's all over."

7
friends and suspects

Several prop people arrived first. Miss Kimberly followed, out of breath. "What's going on here?" she demanded.

Jeri handed over the envelope. "I caught Britney putting this in Lisa's coat pocket." She stared meaningfully into Miss Kimberly's eyes. "I'm guessing it's a blackmail note."

The director gave Jeri a startled glance and tore open the note. Then her whole body sagged. She read it aloud. "Cinderella Celebrates! After Sunday's final performance, come to Britney's dorm lounge for a cast party. Festive food, fabulous fun. Don't miss it!"

The prop people applauded, but Jeri's mouth fell open. It was a cast party invitation?

"Thanks a lot!" Britney spat at Jeri. "A blackmail note? Are you crazy? How *dare* you?" She marched down the row of coats, found Jeri's, and pulled two envelopes from the pocket. "You wrecked the whole surprise. I'm taking back yours and Rosa's. You're *un*invited!" She tore the envelopes in half.

"Look—I'm sorry," Jeri said. "I really am. It's just that—"

Britney marched off to the dressing room, slamming the door behind her. The prop people left, snickering about what they'd witnessed. Miss Kimberly patted Jeri's shoulder. "I can guess what happened here. Are you being blackmailed?"

"No." Jeri bit her tongue, wishing she could mention Rosa's notes. "Actually, I found something you dropped." From her pocket she pulled the note about illegally photocopying music. "I thought Britney's invitation was another blackmail note."

"I guess we can't jump to conclusions, can we?" Miss Kimberly said.

"What will you do about your note?"

"Nothing. Scare tactics don't intimidate me." She rubbed her forehead. "But clearly someone's out to get me. First, we lose our leading lady. And now blackmail." She slapped her hand hard against the wall, and Jeri jumped. "I haven't done anything wrong. I haven't broken any copyright laws."

Shocked—and a little embarrassed—by her outburst, Jeri jammed her hands in her coat pockets and left. She couldn't blame Miss Kimberly for being upset. And if Britney *was* the blackmailer, she'd be on guard now. Either way, Jeri had just managed to get herself and Rosa uninvited from the cast party.

She told Rosa about it when she got back to the dorm. "Don't worry about me. I won't be here then anyway."

"Don't say that! I still have three days to trap the blackmailer before your aunt and uncle come."

"Not really, not with your dad coming for the weekend. But it won't matter. I got expelled for stealing. 'Zero tolerance policy,' the Head said. She means it too — *zero*."

"But you didn't steal any money!"

Rosa rubbed her arms as if chilled. "No, but the Head doesn't believe me."

Jeri rubbed her sweaty hands on her jeans. She just couldn't give up. Rosa had followed her advice about the first note, and it had backfired, leading to the second note. Jeri felt the crushing weight of knowing this wretched situation was her fault.

Before she fell into bed that night, Jeri got an email from her dad.

> Just checking in. I'll be in Landmark Hills late afternoon tomorrow. I'll call your room at 4:30 to make plans for the evening. I've missed you. Dad

Hmm, Jeri thought, *just Dad*. Not "Love, Dad." No "Hi, Sweetie," like Mom wrote. But then, she and Dad weren't exactly close. It was more like having a stranger come for the weekend. *God, please help me get ready for his visit. I don't even know how to talk to him anymore.*

Of all weekends for him to come! If this *did* turn out to be Rosa's last weekend at school, Jeri wanted to spend it with her. She couldn't just leave her sitting alone in their room while she entertained Dad. How would that make her feel?

On Friday morning when Jeri came downstairs, Ms. Carter and a group of girls were waiting for her. The house mother held up a copy of the *Lightning Bolt*. "Listen up, everyone! We have a celebrity in our midst." She pointed at Jeri, who ducked her head. "Her story about the musical made the front page. This is hot off the press!"

Her dorm mates cheered. Ms. Carter cleared her throat and began to read. But her voice faltered as she read Jeri's glowing praise of Rosa's performance. Jeri glanced up the stairs, hoping Rosa was still in their room. But she stood on the top step, listening. Without a word, she turned and walked away. A door down the hall closed softly. A subdued Ms. Carter ushered the girls out the door to breakfast, silently handing Jeri a copy of the school paper as she went by.

Jeri couldn't get Rosa off her mind all morning. Was the blackmailer hiding near the gym, waiting for Rosa's money? Or had she heard that Rosa got expelled and there wouldn't be any payoff? Would the blackmailer still reveal Rosa's secret about her mom?

After school, Jeri dropped off a few books at the library. Dad would be there soon, and her emotions were on a roller coaster ride. One minute she wanted him to come, and the next minute she never wanted to see him again. She'd missed him so much, yet did he have the right to disappear from her life and then pop up suddenly?

Up in her empty room, she was stretched across her bed when someone knocked. "Yeah?"

Abby opened the door. "You ready for your dad?"

"I guess." Jeri turned toward the window. How could she talk to Abby while suspecting her of blackmailing people? Would Abby read the distrust in her eyes?

Abby sat opposite her on Rosa's bed. "Come on, Jer, what's up?"

Jeri shrugged and finally glanced at Abby. The concern on her face melted Jeri, and she propped herself up on one elbow, needing to talk. "Why should I be all excited that Dad's coming after all this time?"

"You're still mad at him?"

"No, not really." At Abby's raised eyebrows, she said, "Honestly! I'm not mad."

"But?"

"But nothing. I forgave him for not being a real dad this past year. I don't talk bad to him. I bought him a Christmas present, even though he never bought *me* one."

"You still sound mad to me."

Jeri resented that. Didn't she deserve some sympathy? "I'm *not* mad. I just don't feel like hanging with him for the weekend."

"Would it be different if he said he was sorry?" Abby asked.

Jeri rolled the idea around her mind. "Yes, but he'll probably pretend that it never happened instead. What if he just makes excuses?"

"What if he doesn't? Don't you want to find out why he's coming?"

Jeri sighed. "I don't know what to say to him anymore." She sat up and glanced at the clock. "It's not too late to call it all off. Besides, I should be spending time with Rosa."

"You don't want to cancel on him." Abby gazed out the window, a haunted look in her eyes. "Life can change without any warning. Make the most of him coming."

Jeri closed her eyes, imagining how Abby must feel. She'd probably give everything she had to see her dad again.

Abby's voice was so soft that Jeri could barely hear her. "I was mad at God for a long time for letting my dad die. I know it sounds weird, but I finally realized that it wasn't God's fault after all." She turned to Jeri. "I hope you'll give your dad a chance."

"You're right," Jeri finally said. "I won't cancel out on him."

"So what are you guys up to tonight?"

"I signed him up for supper at the dining hall, but after that, I don't have a clue."

Jeri waited downstairs in the lounge. Dad had called earlier, saying he needed to shower and change before picking her up. The other sixth graders had already left for the dining hall, and Jeri was grateful. She didn't need an audience for this first meeting.

She planned to forgive Dad if he was sorry. Mom said that forgiveness was the only option, but in Jeri's opinion, Dad should apologize a lot first. Maybe he had a really good reason for staying away all year.

He rang the bell at 5:55 and then knocked. Jeri headed down the narrow, dimly lit hallway to the door. The top of his blond head showed in the half oval of leaded glass near the top. Taking a deep breath, she opened the door.

"Hi, Dad." She stepped back into the hall and stared at the floor.

"So this is Hampton House?" His excitement sounded forced. He wiped his feet on the mat. His loafers were polished, and the crease in his tan pants sharp. Slowly she raised her gaze past his tan coat to his face. His light blue eyes were the same, but his blond hair was shorter, more casual and spiky instead of flat with a straight part. Was that Sabrina's influence? She bristled at the idea.

"Yep! Hampton House." Silence filled the hallway. "Do you want to see it?"

"Sure."

Jeri showed him the lounge, the study room across the hall, the kitchen and breakfast nook, and the deck out back. After each room, he said, "Very nice." She struggled for words but drew a blank.

"How's your roommate? Rosa, isn't it?"

"Yes, Rosa." What could she say? *Well, she was black-mailed twice this week, she almost stole some money from a girl in our dorm, and she's being expelled on Sunday.* "She's fine."

Jeri stared at the area carpet, tracing the pattern with her toe. Part of her was bursting with news to tell Dad: the blackmail notes, the weekly newspaper they published, and her article in the *Lightning Bolt*. The other part of her didn't want to tell him a thing. Not after he'd deserted her all year. Forgiveness or not, shouldn't he have to pay for that? Wasn't that what Mom called sowing and reaping?

"Jeri?" he said softly.

Jeri hesitated and then glanced up.

"I imagine it's been a long year for you," he said. "It's been difficult for me too."

I knew it. Here come the excuses.

He cleared his throat. "I'm sorry I haven't seen you since school started. I've been really busy, but that's no excuse."

Jeri fought back the sudden tears. "You're right. It's not," she whispered.

He shuffled his feet back and forth a couple times. "You're too young to understand some things, but please believe how sorry I am about not being here for you." He cleared his throat again. "Can you forgive me?"

"I already have." Heat crept up her neck and spread across her cheeks. She did *not* want to have this discussion. If he kept going, she'd dissolve into a puddle of tears. "Let's go eat, okay? I ordered you a nice meal at the dining hall."

"So I can eat with you?"

"Yes. When Mom comes—" She cut off her comment, leaving awkward silence.

"Yes, I know your mom's been here more than I have," he said. "She was always a good mother to you."

And she was a good wife *to you!* Jeri wanted to shout. Better than any Sabrina. "Yes," Jeri said. "I miss her a lot." *I missed you too, but that didn't seem to matter*, she didn't say.

Jeri grabbed her coat off the hall tree, slipped it on, and said, "Let's go."

As they strolled across campus, Dad asked questions, and Jeri explained what events took place at the Equestrian Center, what plays the drama department had produced that year, and which sports teams were most competitive. As they walked under a nearly full moon and talked about school, the knot in her stomach gradually relaxed.

The fluttery stomach returned, though, as they climbed the eight stone steps to the dining hall entrance and passed between massive stone pillars into the room with a lofty cathedral ceiling and massive crystal chandeliers. Several hundred girls were already seated and eating.

She glanced at her sixth-grade table where a special place had been set for her dad. Abby spotted them and waved, which made a dozen heads turn in their direction. Jeri felt like an actress in the spotlight—one who'd forgotten her lines. Heat flooded her face suddenly, and sweat beaded on her upper lip.

They sat, and a cook delivered Dad's meal on gold-edged china. Jeri introduced the girls at her table, and Dad smiled and called each one by name. Janine, her long hair drooping over one eye, made a sizzling sound when he shook her hand. Jeri glared at her. This was her *dad*, for Pete's sake. He most certainly wasn't hot! "I didn't even know you had a dad," Janine whispered.

By the end of the meal, he'd charmed all her friends. He asked questions, and they interrupted each other to answer. Part of Jeri was pleased at the attention. She hoped Britney and Hailey noticed what a cool dad she had.

Oddly, though, it also made her mad. They wouldn't think he was so cool if they hadn't seen him all year because he was too busy with his girlfriend. That still hurt. She hadn't been important enough to him to make the effort to see her. She hadn't mattered as much as his girlfriend, and she couldn't pretend the pain wasn't there.

She ate her turkey and mashed potatoes in silence while her friends peppered Dad with questions. Still hungry, she glanced over her shoulder at the dessert table. All right! Cherry pie and brownies tonight, plain or à la mode. She knew without asking that Dad would want the cherry pie with ice cream.

"I'll get the dessert," she said, pushing back from the table.

Miss Kimberly was already there. "Hi, Jeri. You okay after last night?"

"Just humiliated," Jeri said, shaking her head. "I caught a 'blackmailer' handing out party invitations."

"You were only trying to help me, and I appreciate it." Miss Kimberly looked back and forth between the brownies and pie. Finally she took a slice of pie.

"Who's the handsome man at your table?"

Jeri smiled. "Dad's visiting for the weekend."

"I thought so. He looks remarkably like you."

"He does?" That was a surprise. People more often said they didn't look related.

Miss Kimberly glanced at the sixth-grade table. "Is your mom in the restroom?"

"No, she didn't come this time. They're divorced."

"I'm sorry. I didn't know." She added a scoop of ice cream to the dessert. "Is your dad remarried?"

"No." *Thank heavens*, she thought.

"Really?" Miss Kimberly stood tall and appeared to suck in her stomach, but it didn't move. "How about introducing us?"

Horrified, Jeri's mouth opened and closed like a fish out of water. Had she understood Miss Kimberly right? Was the play director wanting to *date* Dad? What a weird idea! "Um, well ... If he had more time ... He won't be here long ..."

Miss Kimberly sniffed. "I understand." She glanced at Jeri's dad again. "Say, I'd be happy to give him a private tour of our historic theater tonight."

"We made other plans already," Jeri said. "Maybe I'll show him tomorrow if we have time." She held out the pie. "I'd better get back before his ice cream melts." She turned to leave, but not before she saw the disappointment in the director's eye.

8
warning

When supper was over, Jeri and Dad walked back to Hampton House with Abby and Nikki. Abby told stories about castles and cathedrals in England. Nikki—who was usually sullen around adults—talked nonstop about her horse boarded at the school.

Back at the dorm, Ms. Carter reminded Jeri that at 7:30 her dad needed to come downstairs to the lounge. She promised, and they all headed up to her room. "Here's Rosa," Jeri said, introducing her roommate.

"Hi," Rosa said. "Glad to meet ya. Hope supper was okay." She patted a stack of books on her desk. "I was working at the library."

Jeri knew that wasn't true, but she just pulled out her desk chair. "Here, Dad." Nikki straddled Rosa's desk chair, and Rosa perched on the end of her bed. Abby sat cross-legged at Mr. McKane's feet, gazing up without blinking. Abby shot him several adoring glances.

Haven't they ever seen a dad before? Jeri thought with irritation. He wasn't *that* handsome! Besides, both Rosa and Abby knew how much his absence had hurt her this year. Where was their loyalty?

At 7:30 they all trooped downstairs to the lounge, where a small fire flickered in the fireplace. Ms. Carter arrived with a tray of sugar cookies and a tiny steaming pot. "Mr. McKane, would you like some coffee?" She set the tray on an end table. "Girls, let Jeri enjoy her dad alone, all right? Take a cookie, but head upstairs with it."

Jeri wanted to protest, *Please don't leave me alone here.* Even if she resented the attention Dad got, it rescued her from having to talk—and from having conversations that could be very uncomfortable.

"Thank you, Ms. Carter," Dad said. "It was nice to meet you all ... Abby, Nikki, Rosa." He nodded at each girl in turn.

Nikki waved, Rosa giggled, and Abby smiled wistfully as they headed upstairs. Ms. Carter returned to the kitchen. Jeri and Dad sat side by side, staring into the flickering blue and yellow flames. The silence lengthened. Jeri munched on her sugar cookie, taking teeny-tiny nibbles to make it last. When it was gone, she'd have to talk.

"You have very nice friends," Dad finally said, break-ing the silence.

"Thanks." *And I couldn't have made it through this year without them, not that you'd care.*

"I'm glad I could meet them," he said.

"They liked you," she said, embarrassed at the edge in her voice.

"That's only because they don't really know me. Right?"

"I wasn't going to say that." *But if the shoe fits ...*

"I suppose you need to go," Jeri said, relieved to end the awkwardness, yet hoping he'd say no.

"It *would* be a good idea to hit the sack early."

"Okay." *Go ahead*, she thought. *Now that my adoring friends are gone, just leave.* She guessed it was too much effort to talk to his own daughter.

Jeri realized that her feelings were all mixed up, but it wasn't her fault that it was hard to talk. He should try harder. Wasn't she worth even that much effort?

At the door, he turned and held out his arms. Jeri felt so torn. Part of her wanted to hold back and show him how it felt not to get what you needed. Her other part longed to make a flying leap into his arms. She settled for a quick hug around his waist.

"See you in the morning, right?" she asked, stepping back.

He smiled. "What time should I be here?"

"Um, I didn't know how early you'd come, so I didn't order breakfast for you in the dining hall. And ... well ..." The meals went on Jeri's school bill, and she couldn't afford to feed him three times a day.

"What if I get a bite at the motel—they have those free continental breakfasts—then come around ten? I'd love a tour of the campus. Then we could have lunch at a diner I saw when I came into Landmark Hills."

"Dale's Diner," Jeri said.

"That's the one. How about it?"

"That sounds good. You'll like the campus. There's a lot to see." She also planned to show him her self-published weekly newspaper and the *Lightning Bolt* article. "'Night, Dad." She shut the door, leaned against it, and closed her eyes.

By 9:40 Saturday morning, Jeri was waiting in the lounge. Hardly anyone was up yet, although she'd heard a few doors slam upstairs and radios come on. At ten, she pulled back the curtain at the front window. No sign of him. Her stomach tightened into a knot.

Was he coming? By 10:15, Jeri decided he'd overslept. At 10:20 she wondered if he'd met someone pretty and forgotten about her. When the doorbell rang at 10:23, Jeri was fighting tears. Embarrassed, she forced herself to smile and went to the door.

Her dad, dressed in jeans and a green pullover sweater, looked fresh and eager for the day. "Hi, honey. Sorry I'm late. I ran—"

"It doesn't matter." Jeri was more curt than she'd intended.

"Yes, it does." He removed his sunglasses. "I ran into a teacher of yours in the parking lot. I don't know how she knew me, but she said terrific things about you."

Jeri cocked her head to one side. "Which teacher?"

"Drama. She said you'd done publicity for her."

"You mean Miss Kimberly?"

"That's the name. She offered to show me the theater, but I said I didn't know what our day's plans were yet."

How embarrassing. Miss Kimberly must have been lurking in the parking lot, waiting for Dad.

Jeri grabbed her coat. "I thought you'd like to see the Equestrian Center first. It has a huge barn and a couple riding rings. It's where I take lessons."

"You ride?" he asked, surprise evident in his voice. "Horses terrify you."

"Not anymore. I got a B in the beginner's class. I'm in intermediate now." She paused. "I'm not like Nikki or anything. She was an expert rider and jumper when she came here. She takes private dressage classes. She practically lives at the horse barn—and smells like it most of the time. She's in competitions with other schools and usually wins." She stopped suddenly, aware that she was babbling like a five-year-old.

Attempting a more grown-up voice, Jeri escorted Dad through the Equestrian Center, the media lab, the sports arena (including the indoor swimming pool), the science lab, the botanical gardens, and the greenhouse. At the clock tower, she pointed at the plaque beside the door. "Our school has one of the few sixty-one-bell carillons in the whole country."

"Impressive! Can you hear the music from your dorm?"

"If the window's open and it's quiet. Somebody plays hymns when the sun sets."

"Can we go inside?"

Jeri shrugged, and Dad tried the door. It was unlocked. Jeri followed him inside. It took a moment for her eyes to adjust to the dimness of the tiny ground-floor room.

"Spooky," Jeri whispered.

"Look. A spiral staircase." Dad moved underneath it and looked overhead. "Want to go up?"

"You can!" Jeri shivered. She'd always been scared of heights.

"Maybe another time then," he said.

Jeri's growling stomach reminded her of the approaching noon hour. Girls would soon pour out of the seven dorms in a rush to the dining hall. She was thankful to be going to Dale's Diner instead.

Over tenderloins and giant onion rings, Jeri finally relaxed. She wished she'd brought some weekly papers and the *Lightning Bolt* to show Dad. She'd do it first thing back at the dorm. If she could avoid Miss Kimberly, she also wanted to show him the theater. Even without a rehearsal to watch, she could show him the orchestra pit, the props and scenery, and the dressing room.

Back in her dorm room at 1:30, Rosa was on the computer. "You guys picked a good day to eat at the diner. We had another mystery meal."

Jeri's dad laughed at her curled lip. "What's that?"

"Last week's leftovers mixed together. The cooks

disguise it by adding a ton of onions." She closed her email program. "See you guys later."

"You don't have to leave." Jeri knew she should say that but still hoped Rosa would go.

"I told Abby I'd watch a movie with her. She's making popcorn now."

Dad tapped the books on Jeri's desk and grinned. "I guess girls don't do homework on Saturdays."

A shadow crossed Rosa's face, and she glanced at Jeri. Jeri gave a small shake of her head. No, she hadn't told Dad Rosa got expelled and no longer had homework to do. Jeri had noticed last night that Rosa's packed boxes had disappeared from sight. They must either be in the closet or stacked in Abby's room.

Rosa grabbed her pink beanbag chair. "You're right. I wouldn't be caught dead studying on a Saturday." She left, closing the door behind her.

Suddenly Jeri was shy. The easy companionship from lunchtime evaporated. "Um, would you like to see my articles?"

Dad didn't answer. He'd carried the framed photos from her desk over to the window. One was the photo of Jeri and Mom taken in their porch swing in Iowa. The other photo was of Jeri and Dad on a camping trip.

"Dad?"

"I remember putting that swing together. It came in a million pieces."

"I didn't know that," Jeri said.

"You were only a baby—maybe two years old." His voice trailed off.

Jeri didn't know how to respond, so she turned on her desk lamp and spread her newspapers out. "This is the media project I told you about," she said, hearing the pride in her voice. "I didn't write all the articles, but I put them all together with Publisher software."

He came to stand beside her and picked up a paper. He read silently, smiled, picked up another paper and read, then looked up. "These are amazing," he said. "What variety: current events, sports, the arts, even an advice column."

"I tried to pattern it after a real paper ... at least a little."

"I bet you got a good grade for this."

"A-," Jeri said. "Abby and I both needed at least a B+ on the group grade to keep our scholarships."

"Abby's the one from England, right?"

"Yup. Her dad died, but her mom works in a museum over there. We both have to study more than Nikki and Rosa to stay in school."

"I'm proud of you," Dad said. "You've accomplished a lot this year."

I'm proud of you. The words echoed in Jeri's head, threatening to make her cry. She quickly pulled out her copy of the *Lightning Bolt*. "This is my article too," she said, pointing to the front page. "I might get to be a reporter. If it happens, I'll be the first sixth grader to work on the paper."

"Remarkable! Let me read your article."

Jeri tried not to smile as he read, but she could see that he was impressed. "Great description of the historic theater here. I had no idea you could write this well."

No, you wouldn't, flashed through Jeri's mind. She clamped down on the thought—she wanted to enjoy the moment—but she couldn't stop the memories flooding her. It wasn't only this school year that Dad had been absent from her life. For two years leading up to the divorce, he'd been away from home a lot. There was a lot more about Jeri that Dad didn't know besides the fact that she could write.

"Well, what now?" he asked.

"Want to see the theater?" Luckily Miss Kimberly could be easily spotted—and avoided, Jeri thought.

As they crossed the campus a few minutes later, Jeri's dad was quiet. "You've changed a lot," he finally said. "You're doing so many things you never did before: horseback riding, learning Publisher, writing for a newspaper ... You've really grown."

"I *have* changed a lot this year." The surge of anger inside Jeri shocked her. "My Sunday school teacher says growth comes from overcoming hard things." She was breathing rapidly, and it wasn't from walking too fast. She had the oddest sensation of being a volcano about to erupt. "I'm different because I had a lot to overcome this year. Being away from home, living with strangers—and having you disappear."

"I know. I'm sorry."

Jeri clenched her fists. "Is that supposed to fix a whole year of forgetting you had a daughter? I never even saw you at Christmas! You were on some cruise."

"I *never* forgot you."

Jeri fought back tears. "Sure seemed like it to me."

Dad waited until four girls passing by were out of earshot. "I can't explain everything that happened this year, but there were circumstances beyond my control—"

"Circumstances like Sabrina?"

"Is that what's upsetting you?" he asked quietly. "I'm sorry you're so hurt—and angry."

Jeri jammed her hands in her coat pockets. "Wouldn't you be?"

Dad walked a few steps away, stared at the administration building, and then walked back. "Let's not talk about this right now. It will just ruin the day for us."

Jeri crossed her arms over her chest. "If not now, *when*?"

"I'd like to come back and see the *Cinderella* play with you. So how about next weekend?"

"You mean if you're not off on some cruise?"

Dad sighed. "Would you prefer that I drove home tonight?"

Jeri stared at the ground. She wanted to say yes and hurt him like he'd hurt her. But she didn't really want him to leave. She wanted him to hug her and say he'd never leave her again and tell her how much he loved her and had missed her.

The silence dragged on.

He sighed again. "I guess I'll go then. I'll call you next week about the play and come back if you want me to."

Jeri slumped. He was leaving and not coming back the next day now. She'd ruined everything, but she didn't know what to do. "Okay," she mumbled, not looking up.

He patted her arm, kissed the top of her head, and then headed toward the parking lot. Jeri fought the temptation to run after him. She waited until he got to his car, thinking he might come back. But he got in, slammed the door, and started the engine.

She watched him drive out of the parking lot and down the hill, where his car disappeared behind a grove of pine trees. She glanced around, hoping no one had witnessed the scene she'd created. Where had all that hurt and anger come from? She'd forgiven her dad months ago—or so she thought. Mom had been gentle, but firm, at Christmas: "Forgiveness isn't a suggestion," she'd said. "It's a command, and it's for *your* good too."

Jeri was sorry now that she'd opened her big mouth. *Please turn around and come back,* she cried inside. She scuffed her shoe back and forth on the sidewalk. *God, why can't I just get over it and move on? Please help me forgive Dad.*

Her heart aching, she trudged back to the dorm. Now what? She didn't feel like joining Abby and Rosa for a movie and answering their questions. Maybe working on her next publicity article would take her mind off Dad. She had plenty of notes on Salli Hall in her role as Prince

Charming. She ran upstairs, but the notes weren't on her desk or in her book bag. What had she done with them?

Then she remembered. She'd had the notebook at rehearsal yesterday when she'd spotted Britney putting the envelope in Lisa's coat pocket. She must have dropped her notebook then. Hopefully it was still near the coat hooks.

Running back downstairs, she jogged toward the theater. At least now it didn't matter if she ran into Miss Kimberly. Of all the nerve today, lying in ambush in the parking lot to flirt with Dad!

Inside the back door of the theater, one dim light burned. Down on her hands and knees near the coat hooks, she peered behind boxes and chests where she might have dropped her notebook. If only she could remember—

"Looking for something?" said a voice behind her.

Jeri jerked and fell over, whacking her elbow on the hard wooden floor. "You scared me!"

Bandana Girl leaned on a broom and grinned down at Jeri. "Lose something?"

Jeri stood and brushed off her jeans. "I dropped a blue notebook in here yesterday."

"I've been cleaning for a couple hours, and I haven't seen it. Lisa was helping me earlier. Maybe she found it." She pointed. "Check the garbage can first. If it's not there, try the prop room. She put a lot of stuff away before she left."

"Okay." Jeri bent over the trash can. "Where's the prop room?"

"Down that hall, first door on the left. Light switch is on the wall."

Jeri rooted around in the garbage while Bandana Girl went back to sweeping. After digging clear to the bottom, she called, "I'm checking the prop room!"

"I'm about done. When you leave, shut the back door tight or the wind catches it. Miss Kim goes ballistic when she finds the door banging."

Jeri hurried down the hallway, dim despite three bare bulbs overhead. She didn't relish being alone in the theater with its spooky echoes, drafty corridors, and props looming in the shadows. The first door on the left was propped open with a paint can.

A light already burned inside. Jeri peered into the room, but no one was there.

A dusty baby buggy, a guitar, and old Christmas decorations were stacked high on a battered desk. Back in the shadows was a poster of *Peter Pan* with a glowing Tinkerbell scattering fairy dust behind him.

Jeri wished she had time to poke around, but she wanted to leave before Bandana Girl. She turned in a slow circle. "Oh, good." She grabbed the notebook from where it lay on a child-sized picnic table. Inside, her notes were still intact.

But something had been added. A hastily scrawled note said, "Want your friends to know your crazy dad was locked up in a mental hospital this year? Keeping this a secret will cost you. Look for instructions soon. Tell no one."

Jeri collapsed on the end of the plastic picnic table, nearly tipping it over. Now *she* was being blackmailed, although no money amount was given. Why split the threat into two notes? Had she interrupted the blackmailer before the note was finished? Most importantly, who would make up such a terrible lie about her dad?

Or was it? Jeri's heart pounded wildly, skipping beats and then thumping so hard her chest jumped. Could this possibly be true? The information in Rosa's blackmail notes had been true. Miss Kimberly's too. Jeri's dad *had* dropped out of sight during the school year. Had he actually been locked up in some mental hospital? Is *that* what he meant by saying she was too young to understand?

Had Lisa written the note before putting her notebook in the prop room? Or had Bandana Girl written it herself? But why? She'd never done anything to them.

Stumbling to her feet, she reached for the light switch. Just then, the overhead bulb blinked off. At the same instant, the prop room door slammed shut. A dead bolt on the outside slid smoothly into place.

9

trapped!

Jeri froze, too stunned to move for a moment. The prop room was totally dark, except for a faint strip of light coming under the door. What was going on? Was this some kind of joke?

She groped for the light switch and flipped it back on. That pushed the shadows back a bit, but the weak light cast an eerie glow on green Peter Pan. Jeri yanked on the knob and then rammed her shoulder against the door, but it didn't budge. Sweat ran down between her shoulder blades. She screamed, pounded with her fists, and kicked at the wooden door.

"Help, somebody! Get me out of here!"

Pausing for breath, she listened for footsteps. Had Bandana Girl left already? The cluttered room wasn't so fascinating anymore. A great place for mice, in fact. She peered into the corners. Or rats.

She pounded and kicked again on the wooden door, screaming till her throat was raw. Within minutes her hands and feet felt bruised. She searched the black, windowless room for a weapon strong enough to break down the door. There was nothing.

Who'd done this to her? Bandana Girl was the only person she'd seen, but anyone could have been lurking around backstage. There were a dozen shadowy hiding places.

Jeri slid to the floor, her back against the door, and stared at the *Peter Pan* poster glued to the opposite wall. A yellow stripe was painted along the bottom edge of the poster. She squinted and stared. Something about it didn't look quite right ...

Wait! Jeri scrambled on all fours across the cement floor. That wasn't a strip of yellow paint under the poster. That was light!

She ran her hand along the jagged bottom of the poster. Sure enough, she could push a finger partway underneath. That huge poster wasn't glued to the wall. It was glued to a painted-over door!

Breathing hard, Jeri brushed her hands up and down the poster, feeling for a knob or handle or some way to open it. At first she felt nothing, but the second time over, she found it. A small metal hook—it felt like a cup hook—was screwed into the door. It was barely big enough to grab hold of. She gripped the hook with her fingers and pulled, but her fingers slipped off. The door remained stuck.

Frantic and fighting tears, Jeri scanned the junk piled on boxes and the old desk. Her eyes slid past and then returned to the guitar. Could she somehow use one of its strings?

She loosened the screw that held the thickest nylon string and pulled it off. She doubled it for strength and then fed it through the metal loop of the hook. Leaning away from the door, she pulled back on the string. The guitar string cut into her skin, so she wrapped a towel around her hand and wrapped the string around and around the towel. She yanked again and again, but nothing budged. Near tears, she pulled hard one more time.

The door popped open an inch, moving the poster. After unwrapping the line from around her wrist, she grabbed the open edge and pulled with all her strength. The door screeched as it swung inward, and Jeri peered down a short hallway. She had no idea where it led, but she had to get out of there. Grabbing her notebook, she headed down the hall. She turned a corner and nearly cried with relief at the big red EXIT sign glowing over a door. She shoved against the bar on the door and practically fell outside.

Standing in the sunshine, Jeri opened her notebook and re-read the note: "Want your friends to know your crazy dad was locked up in a mental hospital this year? Keeping this a secret will cost you. Look for instructions soon. Tell no one."

She studied the handwriting; it looked similar to the other notes. Had the blackmailer locked her in? Or had it somehow been an accident? And what about the message? Her dad in a mental hospital? Had he had some kind of breakdown? If only she could ask him.

Jeri glanced up at the clock tower as it struck five times. She'd originally hoped to catch a movie with Dad tonight in Rock River. Kind of like a date, but not. Jeri sighed, regretting how she'd acted earlier. Why had she been so nasty to him? She'd been sure that she'd gotten over the hurt months ago.

She dreaded going back to the dorm and explaining why she was hanging around on Saturday night, as usual. So she headed to the library instead. She could hide there till nine and read, then just show up back at the dorm. No explanations needed.

After grabbing a magazine, she found a study carrel in a corner of the library basement. But her mind whirled with ideas, and she finally gave up trying to read. She desperately wanted to tell someone about her blackmail note, but who? She usually confided in Abby—but what if *she* was the blackmailer? Or Rosa, but Rosa had her own problems. Her aunt and uncle were coming the very next night to take her out of school.

Jeri dropped her weary head on her folded arms. Everything was such a mess, and she had no clue what to do. One thing was sure though. Time was running out.

On the way to Landmark Hills Community Church the next morning, their school van passed by the motel, but Dad's car was gone. That hurt. Couldn't he have hung around and tried to see her today? She'd invented a story about him having to leave suddenly, but she wasn't sure Abby or Rosa believed her.

She usually loved her Sunday school class, but this morning she couldn't concentrate. Later in church, she felt guilty as she worshiped beside Abby. Jeri sneaked a peek during prayer time. Abby, with her shiny blonde hair and gentle expression, looked positively angelic. *How could I think for one minute that she could be guilty?*

After church, Jeri tried to enjoy the Sunday dinner. Halfway through the salad, a cook arrived with a large tray of covered dishes. "Parent of Jeri McKane?"

Six heads turned to look at Jeri, and her face grew warm. "I'm sorry. Dad had to leave early. I forgot to tell the kitchen."

"Oh." She chewed her lower lip. "I'm afraid you'll be charged anyway since we weren't notified. It's steak and potatoes."

"That's okay."

Nikki leaned across the table. "Since you have to pay for it, can you eat it?"

"I'm not hungry," Jeri said.

"I am!"

The cook grinned and set the tray down on the table. Nikki lifted the silver lids and inhaled. "Ahhh!" she said, grabbing her knife and slicing into the steak. Jeri couldn't help wishing Dad was eating that meal.

Then, abruptly, the cook was back. "I forgot something." She pulled a small envelope from her pocket. "This was left in the kitchen for you."

Jeri's heart hammered. The rest of the blackmail instructions? "Thanks."

"What is it?" Rosa asked. "Open it."

Jeri slipped it into her sweater pocket. "It's just a bill for the food." She forced herself to grin. "I should make Nikki pay it."

"No problem," Nikki said, salting heavily. "It's worth it."

Man, Jeri thought, *it must be nice not to worry about money.* Nikki had the best of everything: leather boots, fancy stuff for her horse Show Stopper, a video phone, a new computer with a copier/printer, her own personal DVD player to watch movies whenever she wanted ... Yes, it must be nice.

While her friends ate dessert, Jeri slipped off to the restroom and hid in a stall to open the note. It was what she'd expected: "Leave $50 tonight at 7 p.m. in the clock tower. Tell no one. Leave money inside a music book."

Fifty dollars? How could she find that kind of money— and by seven o'clock tonight? And should she even try?

If the note was right, Dad hadn't been ignoring her all year or preferring Sabrina over her. He'd been in a mental hospital getting help. If so, she'd been very cruel to him yesterday. The last thing he needed was for the story to be spread around campus. He'd never feel comfortable coming here to see her again.

And yet, she'd told Rosa not to pay, even to protect her mom. Shouldn't she refuse to pay it too? Or ... maybe she *should* pay it—but position herself to catch the black-mailer at the pickup spot.

Walking back to the dorm, she tuned out her friends' chatter to think. She had just six hours to find fifty dollars and hide it in the carillon. But how? No wonder Rosa had been tempted to steal. Jeri glanced at the tower as they walked by and read the concert schedule posted on the door. No one was playing after four o'clock today.

As they turned the corner to Hampton House, Jeri caught a glimpse of Claire, the junior editor, striding toward the library with a friend. Jeri nudged Rosa. "See that girl? That's Claire, the snob in the newsroom I told you about."

Rosa glanced her way. "Looks like the understudy is well now." She sighed. "I guess that's good."

"What understudy?" Jeri asked. "Where?"

"Sarah James. The seventh grader walking with Claire James."

"Claire *James*? You mean the understudy is Claire's little sister?"

"Yeah. Why?"

"No reason." Jeri continued to stare, lost in thought. Maybe the understudy had blackmailed Rosa, or maybe her older sister did it so her sister could play the lead. Claire was mean enough. Or maybe the sisters worked together.

By the time she reached the dorm, Jeri had a plan. Nikki always spent Sunday afternoons at the Equestrian Center, riding or practice jumping. Jeri watched TV in the lounge until Nikki clomped downstairs to leave.

She followed Nikki outside and grabbed her arm. "Can I ask you a big favor?"

"What's up? I'm in a hurry."

"It's an emergency," Jeri said.

"What kind?"

Jeri took a deep breath. "I need fifty dollars, and I can't tell you why. I only need it for tonight. I'll give it right back." At least, she hoped so.

"That's kinda weird." Nikki scraped her cowboy boots on the sidewalk as if pawing the ground. "I guess I could do that," she finally said. "You wouldn't ask if it wasn't important."

"Thanks." Jeri wrung her hands together. "Do you need to go to an ATM?"

"I've got the cash back in my room." Nikki poked Jeri in the arm. *Hard.* "Don't go spreading that around."

"Don't worry. I need you to keep this a secret too— even from Abby." *Maybe especially from Abby,* Jeri thought. "I need it by six thirty today."

"Okay." Nikki studied her watch. "I'll be back around five thirty. I have to put Show Stopper through her paces a couple times before next week's competition."

"Thank you. You're a life saver!" Jeri hugged the taller girl around the waist.

Nikki pushed her away. "Okay, okay." She stomped off, the thudding of her boots fading as she cut across the grass.

Shivering in the breeze, Jeri glanced overhead just as the sun disappeared behind scudding clouds. The overcast sky matched her growing fear.

Jeri fully expected the blackmailer would watch the tower, but she intended to outsmart her. Nikki returned in plenty of time. With the money in her pocket, Jeri arrived at the tower forty-five minutes early. The last scheduled carillon concert was long over.

After circling the tower several times and seeing nothing suspicious, Jeri slipped inside. She moved to the spiral staircase leading up to the tower where there were open windows on all four sides. From there she could spy on the ground below—and see who came to retrieve the money. The circular steps were metal mesh, and partway up was a solid platform. Was the keyboard up there? She couldn't tell.

She climbed up twelve steps to the platform. Pausing, she glanced up, but could only see the next platform. It was already fairly dark, and she shivered. *Don't look down,* she ordered herself, gripping the curved railing. *Just take it one step at a time.*

Taking a deep breath, she climbed higher. She passed the second platform and, with shaking legs, climbed up to the third. Here, enough dim light filtered down from above to reveal an odd-looking keyboard. Rather than piano keys, there were large wooden bars to press and wooden handles hanging on chains to pull. Jeri assumed the chains were attached to the bells in the top of the tower.

On a table near the keyboard were several music books, a hymn book, and some sheet music. Jeri slipped her envelope of money inside the bottom book.

Now, where to hide ... because she intended to stay and put an end to the blackmail scheme once and for all. There was nowhere to conceal herself on this tiny platform though. There was no choice but to keep climbing.

She continued up the last dozen steps to the top of the tower. Crouching below the windows, she crept toward the opening where the clouds were still a bit pink. That had to be west—right over the door below—although the sun had already set. Carefully she rose up and looked out above the trees, then down to the ground. Her head spun. Light-headed and dizzy, she closed her eyes and ducked back down. *Oh, man.* Gradually her head stopped spinning and her stomach settled.

She was right—she'd have a bird's-eye view of the blackmailer when she left the tower. Until then, though, she'd stay down. It was nearly dark, but she couldn't risk being seen hanging out the tower.

Glancing at her watch, Jeri saw she still had at least half an hour before the blackmailer would probably show up. Curious, she crawled around the quickly darkening room at the top of the tower. The humongous brass bells in various sizes were definitely impressive.

Below the bells was a small wooden cupboard built into the wall. Jeri tugged on the loose knob and opened the cupboard. It was empty—except for a giant cobweb. A hairy spider clung to it as it swung gently in the breeze. Ugh! She shivered and backed away.

The wind shifted and blew stronger through the top of the tower. Jeri sat down, wrapping her arms around her bent knees. She wished she'd worn her heavier coat. The floor was cold, and its chill penetrated her jeans. Shivering, she dug in her pockets for her gloves, but found nothing except a quarter and two pennies. She had just checked her watch for the umpteenth time—6:55—when she heard the door below open and close.

Someone's here!

Jeri quietly stood. Why had the blackmailer come before seven? She leaned over the circular railing, listening hard for sounds below.

Faint footsteps. Silence.

Then, ever so slowly, footsteps climbed the circular stairs. One after the other, with long pauses on each platform. Jeri snatched a quick peek over the railing, but didn't see anything. She could hear papers shuffling though.

Just then seven ear-splitting, pounding, thunderous *bongs* filled the top of the tower. Seven o'clock! Jeri gasped and crouched down, covering her ears. She squeezed her eyes shut tightly as if that would somehow quiet the din. Just as the echoes faded, the bells rang out again. Someone was playing the keyboard below, and the bells surrounded Jeri with clanging, piercing, deafening ringing. The racket made her want to scream. Gradually, though, she recognized a song from *Cinderella*.

The publicity! Miss Kimberly had said Britney and some other music students would perform some of the songs this week to advertise the show. Of all times for someone to practice.

Finally, after playing the choruses from four songs, the bells were silent. Jeri finally put her hands down, but the ringing continued in her ears. The only light in the tower now came from a full moon and several security lights nearby.

She tried to stand, lost her balance, and fell forward on her hands. A quarter flew out of her pocket with a *clink*. Holding her breath, she listened hard for sounds below. Was the performer descending the spiral staircase?

No! Heavy, plodding footfalls were coming *up* the last set of circular stairs.

Good grief. Someone was climbing to the top of the tower! Jeri tiptoed to the cupboard in the opposite wall. Taking a deep breath, she swiped at the spider web, now empty. Ugh. Where was that hairy spider? Jeri crawled inside and pulled on the door to shut it. The wiggly knob came off in her hand, so she had to hold the edge of the cupboard door to close it most of the way.

Jeri held her breath. Straining her eyes and ears, she waited for someone to appear at the top of the stairs. Was it Britney? Or maybe Claire? Or—she shuddered—Abby? A minute later, she almost toppled out of the cupboard in surprise when Miss Kimberly stepped into the tower room.

10

starting over

Lord, please hide me. If Miss Kimberly found her, how could she possibly explain being in the tower? The drama teacher might report her to the Head. *Unless I offer to get her a date with Dad,* Jeri thought, almost giggling.

With her finger under the edge of the cupboard, Jeri held the door nearly shut. At first, Jeri could hear her own heart pounding in her ears. Then something tickled her neck. The spider? She shuddered, and her left calf cramped. Jeri held her breath, willing the knot to relax, but it didn't. Moving in triple slow motion, she reached behind and pressed hard on the muscle.

Sounds of several voices floated to her, and at first Jeri thought some girls were passing by on the sidewalk below. Then she realized it *wasn't* several voices. It was just Miss Kimberly, doing the scene where Cinderella was locked in the tower. Was this performance supposed to be publicity? If so, Jeri thought it sounded stupid.

Hurry up! Both her legs were cramping now, and she'd have to move soon.

But Miss Kimberly went on and *on*, even though Jeri could hear her gasping for breath. She even broke into song twice. Finally Miss Kimberly quit. Now, if only she'd leave. Jeri couldn't stand being confined much longer.

Now Miss Kimberly was muttering something. Frowning, Jeri listened closely. What in the world?

She was counting. "... twenty ... thirty ... forty ... forty-five ... fifty. All here."

Jeri peered through the cupboard opening, and her mouth dropped. Miss Kimberly was counting the money Jeri'd left for the blackmailer. She must have stumbled across it in the music book. Now what? She had to put it back for the blackmailer to find!

But wait ... Slowly Jeri recalled the director's words ... *forty-five ... fifty. All here.*

How did she know there was supposed to be fifty dollars altogether? How ... unless she was the blackmailer?

Jeri gasped. Slapping a hand over her mouth, she knocked her arm against the cupboard door. It flew open and Miss Kimberly swung around, the money still in her hand.

Jeri crawled out and stood up. "Hi, Miss Kimberly," she said brightly.

"Good heavens!" Miss Kimberly slipped the money in her jacket pocket. "What are you doing up here? And why are you hiding in the cupboard?"

"Just exploring! The door to the tower was open, so I decided to see what was up here. The sunset earlier was really beautiful." She forced a smile. "I heard you singing. You know the whole musical!"

"I thought it'd be fun to perform the tower scene up here." She cocked her head to one side, and her gaze was shrewd. "I didn't expect an audience though."

Jeri laughed, trying to appear relaxed. If only she could keep her talking. "Um, were you in plays when you were our age?" she asked, inching toward the spiral stairs.

"No, not till high school and college. I studied drama for my major." A grimace twisted Miss Kimberly's face. "I was Cinderella my junior year in our own Rodgers and Hammerstein production."

"Wow! Really?"

"Is that so hard to believe?" Her eyes glittered. "I wasn't always this size, you know."

"I just meant it's no wonder you sound so good."

"Years of experience. Even without Rosa, the musical will be a hit."

Jeri didn't know what to say. Was that why she black-mailed Rosa? To get rid of her and then take over the lead and save the day? Surely not. If she'd wanted to act, Miss Kimberly could have been in the community play.

"It's too bad you don't have time to be in *Oklahoma!*" Jeri said.

"I had the best voice at tryouts." She beamed, but as Jeri watched, the joy drained from Miss Kimberly's face. "That snooty director refused to give me the part though." Her mouth tightened and her eyes narrowed. "Know what she said? That the dancing was too *aerobic* for someone so big—and there weren't any costumes my size." Her eyes blazed, and her hands clenched and flexed, over and over. "The costumes could have been altered to fit me!"

Just like Cinderella's ball gown, Jeri realized. It must have been let out too big on purpose—to fit Miss Kimberly after she got rid of Rosa. She'd obviously never intended for the petite understudy to wear it either.

Miss Kimberly glanced out the tower window. "Is your father still around? I bet he'd enjoy the view of the campus lights from up here."

Dad. If only he were here!

Jeri thought quickly. "He went to his motel for his jacket, but he'll be back any second. He's meeting me here." A car door slammed in the distance. "I bet that's him now. I'll run down and meet him." She turned toward the staircase.

Miss Kimberly stuck out her arm and blocked her way. "So your dad's still here?"

"Yes." Jeri stepped back, an idea forming. "In fact, he said he wants to know you better."

"Really? Funny. I got the distinct impression he wouldn't give me the time of day. When I suggested meeting him, you looked downright horrified. Too hefty, am I?"

"No. Honest. I'm sure he'd like you."

"I agree. We'd make a great couple. Mr. Handsome and Two Ton Tessie." Her teeth gleamed in the darkness. "I mean, he'd be *crazy* to pass up someone like little ole me. They'd *lock him up* and throw away the key."

Crazy? Locked up? Jeri's mind spun. Those were the words written in her notebook. Miss Kimberly *was* the blackmailer. She must be.

Jeri glanced out the window behind her. The campus looked utterly deserted. The dining hall was closed Sunday nights. By now, girls were gathered in their dorm kitchens, making popcorn and pizza. If she screamed, chances were good no one would hear her.

"What's the matter? Scared without all your friends around you?" The director chuckled. "Or were you considering the horror of having me for a stepmommy?"

Jeri knew her eyes were bulging, but she couldn't help it. This psycho woman her stepmother?

Miss Kimberly moved slowly toward Jeri. "Funny thing. I was in the dining hall today. Your friend—the one eating your dad's steak—said he unexpectedly left last night." She paused, her expression hardening like cement. "You lied to me, Jeri."

She opened her mouth to scream, but Miss Kimberly was ready. In one motion, she was behind Jeri. Her hand clamped down, totally covering Jeri's mouth and nose.

Jeri twisted from side to side, trying to scream, but she couldn't breathe. The director was surprisingly strong. She squeezed Jeri around the middle with her left arm while cutting off her air with her right hand.

Light-headedness washed over Jeri. Her knees went weak, and she felt herself being lifted off the ground. She kicked and swung her legs, but couldn't make contact. If only she could get across the tower room and down the spiral stairs! Where was Miss Kimberly carrying her? To lock her in the cupboard? Or—

Oh no, she's going to throw me out the tower window!

Jeri twisted her head sharply to the side. Miss Kimberly's hand slipped enough for Jeri to open her mouth wide. Before she could scream, the director's hand was over her mouth again. This time Jeri bit down on the soft flesh. *Hard.*

Miss Kimberly cried out, and her grip loosened. When Jeri's feet touched ground, she charged toward the stairs. At the same instant, the director grabbed her left arm, and something popped. Jeri gasped. Sharp, white searing pain shot through her arm and shoulder.

She broke it!

Jeri dropped to her knees, holding her left arm close to her body, too terrified and in too much pain to scream. Miss Kimberly blocked the spiral staircase, looming over Jeri in the darkness.

Crab-like, Jeri scooted back. Her hand hit something round and hard. She didn't have to look to know it was the knob from the cupboard. Slowly, carefully, without taking her eyes off Miss Kimberly, she closed her fingers around it.

The director stepped forward into the pool of moonlight, a wicked gleam in her eye. Jeri prayed for a miracle, pulled her good arm back as if winding up to pitch, and let the knob fly. The wooden knob smacked the director in the temple. Crying out, she reeled backwards. She jammed her heel in the mesh of the top step, but her momentum kept her going. She fell down two steps before catching herself against the rail.

At that same instant, the door below banged open. Voices yelled Jeri's name, over and over. She heard Abby's high voice, Nikki's sharp one, and Rosa yelling in Spanish. Then she heard her dad's deep voice! *Thank you, God!*

Jeri screamed again and again. Footsteps pounded up the spiral stairs while Dad continually called her name. Miss Kimberly shook her head as if to clear it. She clutched the railing and pulled herself back up to the tower. Her breathing raspy, she advanced toward Jeri like a steamroller.

Using her good arm to scramble sideways, Jeri scooted until her back hit the cupboard wall. She cradled her injured arm and curled up to make a smaller target.

Arms outstretched, Miss Kimberly lunged at Jeri, her hamlike hands reaching for Jeri's throat. "I'll kill you!" she screamed. "I know what you did to me!"

Jeri screamed, kicking out at the director. Miss Kimberly dropped to her knees, and her hands encircled

Jeri's neck. Jeri twisted back and forth, but it only made the teacher's hands squeeze tighter.

"Hold it!" Dad thundered as his head and shoulders appeared at the top of the stairs. He jumped up the last three steps and threw himself across the tower room at Miss Kimberly.

Grabbing her shoulders from behind, he pulled her backwards. Snarling like a mad dog, she turned and twisted out of his grip. Still on hands and knees, her head down like a bulldozer, she rammed his stomach. Dad staggered, fell, and rolled quickly on the floor.

Abby peered over the top of the stairs. "Get down!" Dad yelled at her.

Miss Kimberly was crawling back toward Jeri, her expression so wild-eyed that Jeri barely recognized her. Her bloated face was red from exertion and shiny with sweat. *What was wrong with her?*

"Dad!"

Miss Kimberly was within arm's reach of Jeri when Dad threw himself down beside the teacher. He grabbed one of her arms and jerked it to the side. She arched her back and kicked out, but missed him. With her free hand, she viciously clawed at his face, leaving two distinct red lines. One slowly oozed with blood.

Dad kept her arm in a viselike grip and twisted it behind her back. She screamed an unearthly scream. Thrashing about, she tried to knock Jeri's dad off his feet.

Finally, cursing, she fell forward on the floor at Jeri's feet, hitting it with a loud *smack*.

Miss Kimberly glared at Jeri, spat, and said, "I'll get you for this!"

Jeri passed out.

Two hours later, they were back in Jeri's dorm room. Dad sat on Jeri's bed, and she leaned against him. Her left arm was in a sling, but the pain killer was taking effect. Her arm wasn't broken, but the torn cartilage would take time to heal.

Her friends' loud chatter confused Jeri, who was still groggy from the medicine. She remembered Miss Kimberly grabbing her around the neck, and she remembered her dad tackling her. After that, there was nothing until she regained consciousness in Dad's arms. He'd been kneeling on the floor of the tower, calling her name.

"Am I dreaming?" she'd asked.

"More like a nightmare," he'd said.

Jeri struggled to sit up. "Where's Miss Kimberly?"

"Lie back. You're safe. She's gone."

Jeri then learned that her dad *had* stayed at the motel, hoping she'd change her mind. When it got dark and she hadn't come back, her friends were worried. Rosa found his cell phone number in Jeri's desk and called him. When Nikki mentioned the $50 loan, Rosa got scared and told Dad about her own blackmail notes. They'd searched then and found Jeri's blackmail note and then raced over to the tower.

Just in time, too …

Across campus, the carillon struck the hour, startling Jeri, and she nestled back against her dad's chest. She'd already told her friends about Miss Kimberly practicing to take over the lead, and how she'd had the dress let out enough to fit her.

"But why target you, Rosa?" Jeri asked now.

Rosa pulled her long hair back from her neck and clipped it on top. "She said I made fun of her about her weight."

Abby rubbed her arms as if cold. "She said a lot of crazy stuff before the police came and arrested her."

Rosa nodded. "She accused me of first insulting her three weeks ago on the first day of rehearsal. When she started to sit on that little stool, I just got her a bigger chair. I didn't want the prop to break. She took what we said about her pretty face the wrong way too. She said we were *really* saying that the rest of her was gross."

Jeri shook her head. "I'm sorry she took our compliments as insults. She sounds paranoid to me."

"That's because you're skinny, Jeri." Nikki balanced her cowboy hat on her knees. "But I get those dumb 'compliments' a lot. Like at horse shows, the judges say that a girl *my size* must have an easier time keeping her horse in line. Or mothers will come up and ask me where I buy my riding outfits because they're very slimming for someone *my size*." Suddenly her faced flushed in embarrassment. Jeri bet that was the most personal thing Nikki had ever admitted.

Jeri glanced at Rosa. "She didn't get a part in the community play either. She lied about that." Jeri related what Miss Kimberly had revealed.

Nikki twirled her hat on her outstretched finger. "So by getting rid of Rosa, she could pay Rosa back for her insults *and* show the community play group that she *could* sing and dance?"

"That's part of it." Jeri's dad shifted his weight and cleared his throat. "Actually, there's more to the story than Miss Kimberly being too sensitive."

Jeri turned toward him. "What do you mean?"

He looked at each girl as if weighing something in his mind. Then he said, "At the hospital—when you went to the vending machines—the doctor came out to talk to your headmistress. Apparently Miss Kimberly's bag held several bottles of pills."

"What kind of pills?" Abby asked.

"One was a prescription drug for calming someone who has huge fears she can't cope with. Apparently if you take this drug, an unfortunate side effect is a huge appetite and often obesity. Miss Kimberly must weigh at least 350 pounds."

Rosa gasped. "Can a person weigh that much?"

"Yes, and that's not all. It appears that in an effort to lose the weight, she was using a second prescription drug. The two drugs taken together had dangerous side effects—including trembling, insomnia, severe head-aches, aggressiveness, and hallucinations." He held Jeri close. "Up in the tower, I think it's fair to say she was out of her mind."

Jeri stared at her bandaged arm, recalling the past week when she'd been around Miss Kimberly. She'd yawned a lot, was dizzy sometimes, and she complained of headaches. "I saw her taking pills once—I thought it was just aspirin. And once I heard her talking to herself in this weird voice."

Rosa shuddered. "You were trapped in the tower with a homicidal maniac!"

"Yes," Dad said. "The police took her to the hospital to check out the lump on her head. She's still under arrest, but she was moved to a psychiatric ward for observation."

"What will happen to her, Dad?"

"I don't know, honey. I can't help feeling sorry for her."

Rosa stood with hands on hips. "Ya know, I feel sorry for Miss Kimberly too, but she didn't need to take out her drug problems on us! If she comes back to school, I won't get near her, even if I'm never in another play."

Jeri glanced at Abby, who smiled and rolled her eyes. The whole forgiveness thing all over again! She herself was getting a lot of practice with forgiving lately: Dad for being absent, Rosa for not trusting her, Miss Kimberly for blackmailing her.

Jeri shifted her weight as her arm began to throb. "Dad, did you know Miss Kimberly blackmailed me because she wanted to date you? She asked me to introduce you, and I made some lame excuse."

Rosa rolled her eyes at that. "One thing I still don't get. How did she deliver the note left under our door? Why didn't someone notice her in the dorm?"

"Because she left the envelope downstairs inside the front door," Abby said. "I saw it when I came back early for a phone call. It had your name on it. I brought it upstairs and stuck it under your door and forgot about it." She shrugged.

"Is Miss Kimberly getting fired?" Jeri asked. "And what about the play now? Is it cancelled?"

"I can answer that," Dad said. "Your headmistress said Miss Kimberly would be on a leave of absence while there's an investigation. I seriously doubt that she'll be back. Drug problem or not, she could have killed someone. Miss Long plans to ask the assistant director for *Oklahoma!* to step in and direct *Cinderella* next week."

"I hope it gets worked out," Rosa said. "I really want to do that play."

Suddenly Jeri remembered that Rosa was supposed to go home that night. "Did your aunt and uncle come?" she asked.

"Yes, they're at the motel where your dad's staying." Rosa grinned and did a fast twirl around the room. "But I'm not leaving! While you were hiding in the tower, Mariah remembered spending the money she thought I stole. She felt really bad for accusing me. My aunt and uncle are going back home tomorrow—without me!"

Jeri grabbed Rosa's arm with her good hand. "That's awesome! I could never have a different roommate."

"I'm on probation, but Head Long was way cool about it," Rosa said. "I'm just lucky she changed her mind."

"Not lucky," Jeri said. "*Blessed*. God is good."

"You're right." Rosa looked around the room. "I'm blessed in lots of ways, starting with all my best friends." She leaned close to Jeri and whispered, "I told them about Mom. Strictest confidence."

Jeri smiled. "You can trust them. I wonder how Miss Kimberly ever found out about your mom anyway? I swear I never told anyone that your dad adopted you."

"I'm sorry I ever said that. During the tryouts for *Cinderella*, you and I were backstage waiting for results, remember? You told me that you'd heard my dad sing once, and I must get my voice from him."

"Oh, yeah!" Jeri said. "I remember."

"I told you that was impossible because Dad isn't my biological father." Rosa sighed. "I guess Miss Kimberly was in the wings because she overheard us. And she was in the park when I went there with Kevin."

It had been easy after all, Jeri realized. Eavesdropping, mixed with resentment and misunderstanding, just waiting for the right time to pay them back. Add drugs to the picture, and anything could happen. In fact, she thought with a shudder, it almost had.

Jeri moved, wincing at the pain in her arm and shoulder. Dad gently rubbed her good arm, occasionally leaning over to plant a kiss on the top of her head. Jeri wished she could stay that way forever, but it was getting late.

He stood carefully. "I'd better go. See you all next weekend for the musical."

Jeri glanced at the clock, surprised to see that Ms. Carter had bent the 7:30 rule. "I'll go with you," she said, wishing she hadn't wasted so much of their weekend being mad.

Downstairs, Dad said good-bye to Ms. Carter and Miss Barbara, who were watching the news on the portable TV in the kitchen. Then Jeri walked him to the front door.

She shifted back and forth from one foot to the other.

"Something on your mind?" Dad asked.

She pressed her lips together and then nodded. "About the note I got ..."

"You're wondering if I was really in a mental hospital this year."

Jeri glanced up. "Were you?"

"No. Miss Kimberly made that up." He pulled her close, careful not to touch her injured arm. "I don't have any such excuse for not coming to see you. And I don't blame you one bit for being hurt and angry. I would be too. But God's been doing some deep work in me this year, and maybe sometime I can tell you about it."

"I'd like that. It's been a big year for me too."

"I can tell. You've grown up so much." He sighed. "I'm just so sorry that I missed some of it. I want very much to make it up to you." He paused. "Can you ever forgive me?"

Jeri nodded. "We can start over—get to know each other again. I'm glad you didn't go home yesterday after all." She hesitated. "When the school van went by the motel on the way to church, I didn't see your car. I thought you were gone."

"I got up early to sit by Sutter Lake and pray. I wanted to be here if you needed me for anything." He leaned back, tilted her chin up, and looked in her eyes. "Because I need *you*."

"Me too." Jeri swallowed the lump in her throat and wrapped her good arm around her dad's waist. She felt the last bit of unforgiving feelings slide away into nothingness. "I love you, Dad."

ZONDERKIDZ